BROKEN ENGAGEMENT

Leonie is hurt and disappointed when Mark tells her they will have to postpone their wedding because he is going to America on a special course for his firm. Hoping to make him change his mind she offers his ring back and to her dismay he takes it telling her she can have it back whenever she wants. Pride will not let her ask for its return and Mark goes to America taking her ring with him.

She moves to Cornwall and meets Justin, an attractive, successful artist who loves her very much, but Leonie cannot forget Mark. But when she met him on his return from America he was most rude to her, so it seems she will have to get over him.

Broken Engagement

by

HILDA PERRY

ROBERT HALE · LONDON

© Hilda Perry 1979

First published in Great Britain 1979

ISBN 0 7091 7694 5

Robert Hale Limited
Clerkenwell House
Clerkenwell Green
London, EC1R 0HT

Printed in Great Britain by Bristol Typesetting Co. Ltd,
Barton Manor St. Philips, Bristol,
and bound by Redwood Burn, Esher

ONE

Leonie Drew heard Mark's laughter before she saw him. When she entered the lounge with his sister Paula, he was with a group of visitors and, as if sensing that someone had entered, he turned, and immediately he saw Leonie the smile left his face.

She watched him anxiously as he left the group and came towards them. "You didn't tell me *she* was coming," he said, and the way he emphasized the she, was meant to show the contempt he felt for her.

Leonie felt the colour fly to her face. "If my presence is going to prove too much for you I'll go," she retorted.

"No need," he said, sarcastically. "I'm sure we can manage to ignore each other."

"Now Mark, don't be objectionable," said his sister. "You don't expect me to give up my oldest friend just because you and she have quarrelled, do you?"

"No. I wouldn't spoil *your* beautiful friendship with Leonie for the world."

He walked away and joined the group he had been with before and talked to them as if there had been no interruption.

Leonie looked at Paula a little distressed. "I knew it was a mistake," she said.

"It was not. We're not going to stop seeing each other just because of what happened between you and Mark. You were my friend before you ever knew him."

"But it's so embarrassing."

"It won't be now you've met again. Just ignore him the

5

same as he intends to ignore you. Pretend he isn't here."

That was easier said than done, thought Leonie. You couldn't ignore Mark. His personality stood out in a crowd. He was amusing and people liked to listen to him, and he was also a successful man whom people felt spoke with an authority they respected.

" Come along, Leonie, you know all my friends, and you're not going to be left out of everything just because you're afraid of coming up against Mark."

That was true. Paula and Leonie had been friends for so long they each knew each other's friends and she was welcomed warmly by Kate, Fiona and Roger, Debbie and Keith, and others who called across to her to join their little circle. Soon Leonie was talking away to them trying to forget that Mark was at the other side of the room talking to another circle of people.

She had arrived for the christening of Paula's little daughter. She was to be one of the godmothers, and she supposed Mark would be the baby's godfather as he was Paula's only brother.

The journey from Cornwall was too far to do there and back in one day so Paula had arranged for her to stay for a long week-end. It was Friday night and she would be here until Sunday afternoon after the christening, that's if Mark Trueman kept his promise and ignored her. She wasn't going to stay if he continued to be objectionable. They had finished with each other and that was that.

But Leonie had regretted quarrelling with Mark. She kept thinking about their quarrel, though she was pretending to be listening to her friends, and she laughed when everyone else did. No one would have guessed that her thoughts were miles away and she was reliving through that last time she had seen Mark.

She had known he would be here for the christening and had accepted the invitation to come herself because she had desperately wanted to see him again, but it was obvious that

6

Mark had got her out of his system and was not pleased to see her. That was not surprising since they hadn't seen each other for nearly two years.

A couple of years ago she and Mark had become engaged and had planned to get married in the summer, but Mark's firm had asked him to go to America to work for one of their units in order to learn all he could about the technical side of the business with a view to becoming the technical manager of his own firm when he returned. It was an offer that came completely out of the blue, quite unexpected.

Leonie had been twenty-one then and had just become established in her own hairdressing salon. She had been most upset and angry when Mark said he was accepting this opportunity to go to America. His job wasn't bad and with her business too, she didn't feel it was that important for him to put off the wedding in order to better himself.

" We can't put off the wedding," she protested. " Everything's arranged."

" Do you think I haven't thought of that, darling?" he said. " I don't want to put our wedding off, but you must see, love, that if I am made technical manager of my firm it will lead to other promotions and we shall have a very secure future ahead of us. I just can't afford to miss the opportunity. You want your husband to be in a good position, surely?"

" You are so ambitious you would postpone our wedding?" she cried.

" Well, don't put it like that," he answered, angrily. " I've told you I don't want to postpone the wedding, but I have to think of our future. This is too good an opportunity to miss. Surely you can see that."

" No I can't," she snapped, terribly disappointed because her wedding was to be put off. She had made plans and it was the uppermost thing in her mind every day when she awoke, and she just couldn't bear it if she had to wait until Mark returned from America. There would be other opportunities if he turned this one down.

"How long would you be away?" she asked.

"About a year."

"A year!"

"That will soon go, you'll see."

He seemed so complacent about it that she accused him of not being in love with her at all. "If you were, you couldn't bear to go any more than I want you to," she cried.

"If you loved me you would be more understanding. You're being selfish in not seeing what this opportunity means to me."

"Well, all right, if that's what you think. I don't have to wait for you until you decide to come back from America. I could get married tomorrow. Eliot Warner wanted to marry me before I met you and he still does."

Leonie had only been trying to make Mark jealous and trying to get him to change his mind about going abroad, but when she said Eliot wanted to marry her he snapped, "Well go ahead, marry Eliot."

She had been so flabbergasted that he could say that that she had just stared at him. "Well I will," she said, defiantly. She took off her engagement ring and handed it back to him, confident he wouldn't take it, but he had taken it. "If you change your mind let me know," he said.

Then he had taken her home and they had travelled in silence all the way. "Do you want me to kiss you good night?" he asked, when they reached her home.

"No, you needn't bother," she said. But she had prayed he would accompany her to the door and kiss her good night in spite of her refusal, but he hadn't.

He held up their engagement ring and said, "You can have it back whenever you want it."

But with her head held high she had marched away and went indoors without a backward look. As soon as she had got indoors she had fled upstairs and cried her heart out. Mark didn't love her. He couldn't have let her go like that

8

if he did.

Stupidly the next evening she had told her mother that if Mark called or phoned she was to tell him she was out with Eliot. Then she'd gone out to the pictures all on her own feeling as miserable as sin. She had wanted to punish Mark for being so unaffected by her giving him back his ring, but now she wished she hadn't been so hasty. She shouldn't have gone off the deep end as she had done. It was just that she had been so disappointed about her wedding having to be postponed. Mark couldn't afford to let an opportunity affecting his future go by and she had been most unreasonable. She knew that the income coming from her hairdressing salon together with Mark's wages would keep them comfortably which was okay until she started a family and then she'd have to give up work and they wouldn't be able to give their children the best in life unless Mark had a well-paid position. She couldn't sit through the film she felt so unhappy and half-way through she went back home. Her mother told her Mark had been and she'd given him the message.

" What did he say?" asked Leonie.

" He seemed most surprised. He thought I was joking."

" Did he leave a message for me?" she asked.

" No. He just stood there as if he couldn't believe you were out with Eliot. Why did you have to see him?"

" I didn't. I only told you to tell Mark that because I wanted to get my own back with him. We had a quarrel last night and I thought it might be a good idea to let him see that there were other fellows interested in me besides himself."

Leonie didn't tell her mother the reason for their quarrel for she knew she would have taken Mark's part. She rang Mark's home but there was no reply and to her horror she learned the next day that Mark had boarded a plane for America. He had gone without attempting to get in touch with her again. She was stunned. For one thing she hadn't

9

realized he was going so soon, and for another she couldn't believe he could go without insisting on seeing her and giving her back her engagement ring.

Shortly after he had arrived in America he had sent her a short letter saying it was a good thing he had discovered about her and Eliot before it was too late. " You had me fooled," he wrote. " I really thought I was the only man in your life. Never mind. I have been allocated a really dishy secretary and I'm sure she'll be willing to console me."

Leonie had been tempted many times to write and tell him she wasn't in the least interested in Eliot. It was true that he had asked her to marry him more than once, but it was Mark she loved, and he had been so flippant about the ending of their engagement she just couldn't write and tell him how much she loved him.

She had been terribly unhappy and her mother and friends couldn't understand why she and Mark had split up : " You were so suited," said her mother.

For a time Leonie actually did go out with Eliot but she had made it quite clear to him that she did not want to marry him even though she enjoyed his company. If she couldn't have Mark she didn't want anyone, she told herself, and not even Paula, Mark's sister, knew how heart-broken she was over losing her brother.

To add to her misery she had discovered that she was allergic to the chemicals used in the hairdressing business. Her hands began to break out in dreadful rashes and her doctor advised her to take up a different occupation.

This was quite a blow for Leonie as she had always planned to be a hairdresser and when she had her own hairdressing salon bought from the money her father had left entirely to her, she had been delighted. She was not sufficiently established to leave the salon in charge of a manageress and had had to sell up.

Mrs. Drew suggested they went down to the Cornish coast to stay with her sister who had recently lost her husband. " Louise is always asking me to go and make my home with her. It would be nice for us to be together, for a time, at least."

Leonie agreed that it would be a good idea for her mother to stay with her sister for a time to see if she could be contented in Cornwall and she had accompanied her. Aunt Louise lived in a large three-bedroomed bungalow and had been delighted to have them with her. Leonie's mother had been so happy she had asked her daughter to return to the Midlands and sell up their home and its contents as she intended to stay with her sister.

Leonie learned from Paula that Mark had returned from America looking tanned and well, and shortly after his return he was made a director of his firm. He was doing extremely well. Leonie realized he had been right to put his job before everything. A year had soon passed now it was over, but it had seemed a long time going while he was abroad. In fact it seemed only like yesterday that she had given him back his ring and spoilt everything for herself.

Early in the year Paula and her husband Ron had stayed for a holiday with Leonie in the bungalow she and her mother were sharing with her aunt. Her mother's room had two single beds and Leonie was able to move into her room temporarily. Paula had been pregnant then. " You must come to the christening," she said. " I want you to be the baby's godmother."

And so here she was and there was Mark, better-looking than ever. He had always been tall, and now he had broadened out and looked quite distinguished. He had changed in nearly two years. It seemed he had changed from a boy into a man, and she felt she had changed from a girl into a woman. She found herself glancing in Mark's direction all the time, but never caught him looking in hers. He wasn't the slightest bit interested in her.

Well, had she expected him to greet her with open arms and tell her all was forgiven and that he carried her engagement ring with him wherever he went hoping that someday he could give it back to her? No, she hadn't quite expected that, but she had hoped he would at least speak to her, and as he didn't seem to be attached to any particular girl, according to Paula when she was in Cornwall, she had hoped they might get together again.

Paula had prepared a buffet for her guests and as the evening progressed they began to help themselves. Leonie felt she couldn't eat a thing and stood empty-handed while everyone around her was piling up their plates. She watched Mark helping himself and others at the same time. In fact she could hardly keep her eyes off him. He was wearing a light beige suit with chocolate brown shirt and beige tie. His thick light brown hair was streaked with gold as if he had been in the sun and it had bleached in parts. His gold wrist watch shone on his tanned wrist and she looked at his well-shaped hands which had once been so familiar to her. It was difficult to believe that she had sat at concerts and in the cinema with her hand held closely in his. That they had walked hand in hand over commons and through the woods. As if sensing her eyes upon him he looked up and seeing she was not eating, nor had she a plate, he said, " Aren't you going to help yourself?"

She met his deep blue eyes for a moment and then her own faltered and she looked away. " I'm not hungry," she said.

" I hope my presence hasn't spoilt your appetite," he said, sarcastically.

She shrugged and walked away. If he only knew how much his presence had affected her appetite. She hadn't realized how much she had longed to see him again until now and it was no good. After two years she had been able to forget him for long periods at a time, but she had never completely got over her loss for she never felt drawn to any other fellow. Even if she did make a date with anyone she knew no one could ever mean so much to her as Mark had done,

12

and she didn't want anyone to mean more. In her heart she had always been true to him.

Her presence didn't seem to be affecting him at all for he was laughing and talking the same as he'd been when she arrived. However, he apparently went to Paula and told her that one of her guests was not helping herself for soon Paula came along and gave her a plate full of all the good things she knew were her favourites. "There," she said. "Mark said I was neglecting my guests, but you aren't like an ordinary guest are you? You're one of the family, almost. I told Mark you would help yourself when you were hungry."

Paula and Ron had plenty of dance music on tape and when everyone had finished wining and dining some of the couples began to dance. Leonie had the humiliation of seeing Mark dance with almost every girl in the room except herself. She was claimed by several young fellows, and laughed and danced as if she hadn't a care in the world, but she was hoping, yet dreading that Mark would ask her to dance, and the disappointment when the evening ended and he hadn't asked her for one dance was almost more than she could bear. How he must hate her, she thought.

She went to the bathroom to hide her disappointment and saw that her eyes looked wide and dark. Sea-green eyes stared back at her and she saw that her face was very pale. She was wearing a floral dress with a matching bolero. She had always felt good when she wore this outfit, and yet Mark had completely ignored her all the evening. It was insulting. She wished she could leave, but Paula would be upset. And why should she let Mark affect her? She would let him see she couldn't care less whether he spoke to her or not. He was rude. He could at least have treated her as just a guest, and a guest wouldn't expect to be ignored.

She returned to the party with a bright smile fixed on her face and was immediately claimed by a young fellow who had taken quite a fancy to her. His name was Rex and he

13

had been drinking heavily all the evening. She looked at him and saw that his eyes were bleary. Oh, God, she wished she could leave that very minute. He tried to kiss her and it was then that Mark intervened.

" Sorry old chap," he said. " The party's over. You aren't driving, are you?"

" No," said Rex, " I'm with Steve."

" That's good," said Mark. " You couldn't drive in the state you're in."

He drew Leonie away from him. " You look tired," he said. " I expect you could have done with a quiet evening after driving here from Cornwall."

" I'm all right," she said. " Nearly everyone has gone now and I can't say I shan't be glad to get into bed."

At that moment Paula's husband joined them. " Yes, you are tired, Leonie," he said. " It was unfortunate that you walked into a party after your long journey. We invited this crowd some weeks ago without realizing that it tied up with the christening weekend and it's been hard work for Paula. But they've nearly all gone and you can go and tuck yourself up in bed. You needn't get up early in the morning."

" Thanks, Ron," said Leonie. " I feel as if I could sleep forever."

She liked Ron and his kindness made her feel near to tears after being so rudely ignored by Mark all the evening.

Paula took her up to the room she would be using while she was here as soon as the last guest had left. " You'll sleep like a top," she said. " You look all in."

Leonie thanked her for everything and when she'd gone she looked round the room appreciatively. It was a very pleasing one decorated in lavender and white. There was a bathroom *en suite* also done out in lavender and white. Tired as she was Leonie lifted the curtains to one side and looked out across the garden to the landscape beyond. Paula certainly had a lovely home in beautiful surroundings. Ron was an accountant doing extremely well by the look of things. They

14

lacked for nothing in their beautiful home.

Leonie prepared for bed and sank into its luxurious soft-
ness. She expected sleep to come quickly she was so tired,
but she couldn't. She could only remember how stupid she'd
been a couple of years ago when Mark had told her he had
to go to America. She could see more than ever how unreasonable she had been. A man had to look to his future
and she'd been very childish expecting him to let a wonderful opportunity go by just because it meant postponing their
marriage for a few months.

If Mark hadn't departed so quickly she would have had
time to simmer down, get over her disappointment and let
him know that she knew she had been stupid, but there had
been no time for that and just for her short period of pique
because her wedding was to be delayed she had had to suffer
and lose the man she loved.

Seeing him again had brought back all the old heartache,
even more so, because Mark had changed. He seemed so
much more a man, and a distinguished one at that. She could
imagine him being on the board of directors and discussing
important affairs with his colleagues.

Her eyes ached and smarted for want of rest, but sleep
evaded her until it was almost light and then when she was
beginning to think she would never get any rest she sank
into a deep sleep and didn't wake until nearly midday. It was
a question if she would have awoken then, but she heard a
movement and opened her eyes to see Paula moving softly
towards her to see if she was awake.

The sun was pouring into her room and she looked at
Paula in dismay. "What time is it?" she asked.

Paula laughed. "No need to look so guilty. You've slept
well and I wouldn't disturb you."

"But it's so late."

"Well, you are just in time for lunch instead of breakfast," laughed her friend.

"Oh, dear!"

15

"It's a wonder you didn't hear Samantha yelling this morning, it was enough to waken the dead, she does let go."

Leonie smiled. "She's a lovely baby, Paula, I envy you."

"We're chuffed to death, Ron and I," said Paula, going to the door. "I'll just go and fetch you a cup of coffee and some toast to keep you going until lunch time which won't be long."

"Now don't bother," said Leonie. "You have enough to do without waiting on me. I can quite easily wait until lunch."

Paula ignored her and went downstairs. Leonie, feeling guilty about staying in bed so long hurried into the bathroom. She would give Paula a hand to make up for lying in bed so late.

This morning everything seemed so bright and lovely in Paula's home. She hadn't imagined Paula lived in a home anything near so grand as this. She was pulling on her tights when Paula returned with a tray and she looked up at her reproachfully. "Oh, Paula, I told you not to bother."

"It's no bother. Samantha is sleeping peacefully and I have everything under control."

"Is Mark staying here with you?"

"No. Didn't I tell you? He has a very nice house quite near. He had it built to his own design."

"He's getting married soon then?" Leonie felt the ache in her heart as she asked.

"Well I think it's time he did, don't you? There are two girls in particular he sees and I can't make up my mind which one he is most keen on. The one is his secretary, she seems very efficient, and he relies on her a lot, and then there is Josy. She's rather nice in a sweet sort of way. I can't imagine Mark married to her, but he seems to think a lot of her." Paula looked at Leonie, consideringly. "I can't imagine why you and Mark called everything off. You both seemed so fond of each other. Mum and Dad and I couldn't believe it when he said the wedding was off, and he flew to America

16

immediately after telling us."

" It was because he was going to America that we quarrelled," said Leonie. " It all seems so stupid now, but I was upset when he told me he was going abroad and our wedding would have to be postponed. I made a terrible fuss and said he was putting his job before our happiness. I told him I could marry Eliot Warner any time and he told me to go ahead. When he called for me the next night I was out and I told my mother to tell him I was with Eliot."

" And were you?"

" No. I've been out with him since, but I didn't go out with him that night."

Paula looked at her thoughtfully. " And I suppose Mark thought you really meant it about marrying Eliot?"

" I suppose so. I would have told him there was nothing in it at all, but he went off to America almost immediately, as you say, and then I had a letter from him—very brief— and he said he was being consoled by a dishy secretary out there."

" You stupid pair," declared Paula.

" Oh, well, we were younger then. We've both got over it by now. It's obvious that Mark doesn't even like me any more, so it wouldn't have done for us to get married when one quarrel could turn us against each other so much."

" I suppose it was understandable that you should get upset about having your wedding postponed. I would have felt just the same. Mark wasn't very reasonable to let your protests end everything between you and not make any attempts to persuade you to wait for him."

" When I gave him his ring back he told me I could have it back whenever I wished, I only had to say."

" Stupid idiot. He should have known that your pride wouldn't allow you to ask him to give it back to you."

" It just shows that his feelings for me weren't all that deep."

" I can't believe that. Mark isn't one to take anyone's

17

affection lightly. Of course he went off to America and none of us had the opportunity to see whether he was upset or not. Have you ever thought of asking for your ring back?"

Leonie laughed. " Goodness me, no!"

" Why not ask him and see what happens?"

" He would either be most embarrassed, or he'd tell me where I got off. I don't want it back now," she lied.

" No, I suppose you've had time to get over it. I should like to hear that you'll be getting married soon, Leonie. You and I are very much alike, and I think there's nothing to beat married life."

" If I meet someone like Ron I'll give it a try," smiled Leonie. " Men today are not so keen to tie themselves down. They can get what they want without marriage."

" They're not all like that. Ron didn't expect anything from me until we were properly married and you know, Leonie, when we got married it was lovely to go on our honeymoon knowing we had that to look forward to. It would take all the thrill out of marriage if you had all the sex you wanted before."

" I'll have to wait until that sort of man comes along," laughed Leonie, taking up her coffee, and nibbling her toast.

" I have a lot of shopping to do and my blessed car won't go. I'm waiting for Ron to come home so that I can borrow his."

" I'll look after Samantha for you, shall I?"

" I was hoping you'd come with me. I can put Samantha in her karricot in the car and then she's only a tiny mite to carry round while we do the shopping. There's lots of things I have to get for the party after the christening tomorrow."

" I'm surprised Ron has to work on a Saturday."

" Oh, people who work for themselves work much harder than those who work for a boss, believe me. Ron is doing extremely well, but he works a good many hours. It's nothing for him to sit until midnight after a hard day at the office."

18

" And you don't mind?"

" Well, I mind. But it's his job. We like a good standard of living and Ron has to work hard for us to have it. A lot of people might envy us, but believe me Ron has put his job before everything."

Paula went down to see if Samantha was all right and Leonie couldn't help thinking how differently Paula had behaved to herself. She had resented Mark putting his job before their wedding and because of that she'd lost him. He was in a good position now and someone else would benefit when it could have been herself.

If she was going shopping with Paula she decided she might as well get ready for going out now for if Paula had a lot of shopping to do the sooner they went the better. It was a glorious day and the weather seemed settled so she decided to risk going without a coat. She had a lovely satiny silk turquoise dress with a pleated skirt. She was very slim and it suited her, though she often felt that pleated skirts made one look fatter. It was a dress that didn't crease and for that reason she had put it in her case.

When she went down Paula was looking harassed. " You know what? Ron has just rung to say he won't be able to get home until later this afternoon. I told him my car won't go and I reminded him of all the shopping I had to do, but he just can't make it. He has a very important client and can't get away."

" Well I'll look after Samantha while you go on the bus," Leonie was saying, when they saw the kitchen door open and Mark entered. They hadn't heard his car.

" What's this about going on the bus?" he asked.

" Oh, Mark," cried Paula, " am I glad to see you. My car won't go and I've such a lot to do. Ron't got to work late— do you think you could have a look at the car and see what's wrong?"

" Not in these togs," he said. " I came round to see if there was anything you wanted me to do such as getting

19

some drinks in," he grinned, " but I'm not in the mood for looking at your old wreck. I'll run you into town if you like."

" Can you wait until I've fed Samantha and we've had our lunch?"

" I suppose I could if you offer me some lunch too."

" I think we can make it stretch to one extra," she said.

" Can I help?" asked Leonie.

" You could give Samantha her bottle while I see to the table."

Leonie went out to Samantha who had just started to cry in her pram in the garden, and she lifted her gently. She went indoors cradling her in her arms. Mark had followed her out and as she looked down at the baby he had stood behind her looking too.

" She's a little beauty," he said.

Leonie felt the tears start to her eyes. Samantha was so lovely, and she could see that Mark would be a wonderful father when he had children of his own, for he obviously adored his sister's little baby.

TWO

Samantha was angelic when her stomach was full, but now she was hungry and she changed from an angelic little mite to a yelling little demon. Her face grew red with anger because there was no food forthcoming immediately and she kicked and screamed for her bottle.

Laughing, Mark took her from Leonie's arms, "You haven't got the right technique," he said, and held the baby against his shoulder. She looked like a little kitten against his broad chest. He was mistaken in thinking she would stop yelling for him, for she continued to get herself hot and bothered until at last he handed her back to Leonie.

"Here, you can have her," he said. "She's typical of all women. They all go mad when they can't get their own way."

"I expect you yelled even more than she is doing when you were waiting to be fed as a baby," retorted Leonie.

"It's too far back for me to remember," he grinned.

Paula appeared with the baby's bottle and they all went indoors to see that Samantha was appeased. "Let me give it to her," pleaded Leonie.

"Right. Get comfortable in this chair and be prepared to have a lot of patience. She'll go at it like mad for a bit, and then she'll get lazy and take her time."

The three of them watched in fascination as Samantha fastened her tiny mouth greedily on the teat and almost choked herself after the first few gulps. And then, with satisfied little grunts, she sucked steadily without stopping

21

for breath.

Leonie didn't realize how tenderly she was looking at the little mite in her arms. She looked up to see Mark watching her with a strange expression. She met his eyes for just a fraction and then lowered her own. Was he thinking, like herself, that if they had been married when they had planned they too could have had a little daughter or son, the same as Paula?

Paula had been busily putting the last touches to the table and she paused now to look at Samantha. " Put her over your shoulder, Leonie, and get the wind up for her. She's taken it too quickly," she said.

The baby's mouth closed firmly on the teat as Leonie tried to take it away. " She doesn't intend to let go," she said.

" She must," said Paula, and went forward to take the bottle away, whereupon Samantha let out an angry yell.

" It's for your own good, darling," said Paula. Leonie, very awkwardly lifted her to her shoulder and rubbed her back. The wind came up with a great gurgling sound which made them all laugh, and then Samantha was ready to start on her bottle again.

She was not so greedy now, and gradually she began to doze over the feed. " Don't let her go to sleep over it," said Mark. He had obviously watched this performance before.

Leonie wriggled the bottle in her mouth and she took a few half-hearted little sucks, and lay back in Leonie's arms perfectly contented with little smiles flickering across her face. " Oh, look! She's smiling."

" That's wind," said Mark. " It makes them look as if they're smiling."

" Oh, I'm sure it's not," said Leonie. " See how contented she looks."

It was obvious she did not intend to finish her bottle right now so Paula took it away and lay Samantha in her karricot. " Now just you be good," she said. " You've had your lunch and it's time we had ours."

" I hope I'm not putting you out too much, Mark," said Paula, as they took their seats at the table.

" I'll forgive you seeing as you're providing me with this very excellent meal," he said, pleasantly.

" Perhaps you could give Ron a ring and ask him what drinks he wants you to get, if that's what you really came round for."

" Good idea. I can go and see to that while you are busy with your shopping."

" Ron would have to work on a day when I need his help."

" Unfortunately a man has to put his job before everything else," said Mark, and he looked at Leonie quite sure she would understand that he was referring to her unreasonable behaviour because he had done just that.

" I know I should be grateful," said Paula. " If Ron was short of clients it would be far more worrying than having too many."

When they had finished their meal Paula changed Samantha and gave her the remainder of her bottle while Leonie and Mark cleared away and washed up.

Leonie was very conscious of Mark standing there beside her taking his time as he dried each item and put it away. He whistled softly as he worked making no attempt to talk to her. He showed no curiosity about where she was living or what she was doing. He made it quite clear that he was completely indifferent towards her.

Today he was wearing light trousers, well cut with a mustard-coloured jumper—casual clothes, but he still looked as handsome as he'd done last night. She looked at his well-shaped hand as he reached out for another dish and wondered what his reaction would be if she carried out her longing to put her own over his and let him know how much she wished they would start all over again.

" I hear you have a house built for yourself," she said.

23

He stopped whistling. " Yes. It's all finished and ready waiting for my wife."

Her heart sank. So he had someone in mind.

" I expected to find you married to Eliot when I returned. Didn't he come up to scratch, either?"

She winced at his sarcasm. " I never wanted to marry Eliot," she said.

" No?" he asked, raising his eyebrows. " You gave me the impression you preferred to marry him rather than wait a few months longer to marry me. But he wasn't so eager as you thought, obviously, so you were left with no one. I suppose you have someone eagerly waiting for you down in Cornwall, though?"

She didn't answer and he said, " What made you sell up your shop and go so far away."

" I had my reasons," she said, coolly.

" To get as far away from me as possible when you knew I was coming back home?"

She gave him a troubled look. " It wasn't like that at all. Anyway, you wrote to say you were being consoled by your dishy secretary."

" Oh, sure," he said. " I had a marvellous time in America."

He placed the towel down. " I'll go and give Ron a ring and see what he wants me to get for tomorrow."

Leonie finished wiping the remaining dishes and tidied the kitchen. She had been hoping that meeting Mark again would either convince her that she no longer loved him, and could get him out of her system for good, or it would bring them together again, that she would find he still loved her. But it wasn't turning out that way. She was still in love with him, but he obviously despised her.

He was a more mature person now that he was so success-ful at his work, and she could see that it had been necessary for him to consider his future. Mark wouldn't have been satisfied with a mediocre job. It would have been a shame

24

if he had given in to her and refused to take the opportunity his firm had offered him. But she would have given in and accepted the fact that it was in her interest as well as his own that he get the experience required of him if only there had been more time. He had been whipped away from her so quickly. She had given him the impression she had gone to Eliot and there had been no chance to tell him it wasn't true.

But if his love for her had been as strong as he reckoned it was, surely he would have written to tell her how he felt about her going with Eliot and he would have begged her not to leave him for someone else. He hadn't been very understanding when they quarrelled. He could have asked her first how she felt about his going abroad instead of announcing that he was going before even discussing it with her. He had been insensitive too, she told herself, as she threw down the dishcloth and turned from the sink. He should have known how disappointing it would be to any girl to learn that her wedding was to be put off, but he had made no allowances.

Well, now that she had seen him again and knew that there was no love in his heart any more for her, perhaps had never been all that much, she would return home and put him out of her mind for good. She had been stupid to hope there might be a reconciliation after all this time. Now that Mark was in such a good position he would require a much more sophisticated person for his wife than she was, anyway.

She slipped off the apron she had put on to protect her frock while washing up, and then slipped to the bathroom to see that she was looking okay. She gave her hair a comb through, it was easily manageable hair with just sufficient natural wave to save her having to get a perm. When she went down Samantha was peacefully sleeping in the karricot on the back seat of the car and they were waiting for her.

" Sorry if I've kept you waiting," she said.

" No, you haven't, we're only just ready. Would you like

25

to go in the front and I'll squash on the back seat by Samantha."

" I don't mind squashing on the back seat," said Leonie.

" Oh, for goodness' sake get in," said Mark, impatiently. He didn't seem so good-humoured now and Leonie hurriedly got in beside him, but she was very quiet all the way to town. She couldn't help thinking of all the times she had sat at his side in a car much shabbier than this present one, and how happy they had been in those days.

Paula in the back was busy studying her shopping list and deciding which store to go to first. Mark parked on the nearest car park he could to the shops so that they wouldn't have far to walk with their groceries for they were having to carry Samantha as well. She was far too tiny for a push chair at this stage.

" I'll take her," said Leonie, as they lifted her carefully from her cot, and she cradled her gently in her arms so that she wouldn't wake.

" Where shall you be?" asked Mark. " When I've finished my shopping I'll look for you and help you carry yours."

Paula told him which shops she was going to, and they set off. " We shall have to hurry," said Paula. " I've a lot to get and Samantha will be ready for her next feed probably before we get back and we know how she'll yell when she's hungry."

They soon began to load the shopping bags and Leonie was finding Samantha quite heavy for all she was such a little scrap. It was a warm day and she was thankful she was not wearing a coat for she was beginning to feel extremely hot and sticky with the baby's warm little body pressed close to her own.

Just as she was feeling she would have to beg Paula to take a rest, Mark came striding towards them. He took one look at her face which was as red as a turkey cock, and immediately relieved her of the baby. She looked ridiculously small in his strong arms.

26

" Done your shopping already?" asked Paula.

" Yes, it's in the boot of the car. Let me take one of your bags."

" I can manage," she said. " It's a great help if you'll hang on to Samantha for us."

They bumped into a friend of Mark's who grinned when he saw the baby in his arms. " Ah, you make a wonderful father," he said.

Mark didn't mind at all being caught holding the baby. " You have to give the ladies a helping hand at times," he grinned.

" I think I've got all I want now," said Paula, about half an hour later, and they all gave a sigh of relief, and made their way back to the car.

" I would suggest calling somewhere for a coffee," she said, " but it will be Samantha's feeding time soon."

" Well let's get home before she starts," said Mark, putting her down carefully into her cot.

Back at the house Mark stayed for a coffee and then said he'd be off. " I've got a date for tonight," he grinned.

" Well thanks a lot, Mark," said Paula. " I don't know what we'd have done without you. Ron will settle up with you for the drinks when he sees you."

" That's okay. See you tomorrow for the great event then," he smiled, and they watched him zoom away.

Leonie was glad to help Paula sort out her shopping for it seemed so dead now that he'd gone, and it helped her to stop thinking about the date he had that evening.

" Mark's a good sort," said Paula. " You wouldn't get many brothers who'd help a sister out as he's done today, would you?"

" No you wouldn't," Leonie agreed.

Ron came home looking tired and Paula fussed round him, getting his slippers and making him a drink. " I'm sorry I got so tied up today when there was so much for you to do, love," he said.

27

"We managed," said Paula. "I've had Leonie and Mark to help, thank goodness."

When he went into the kitchen and saw all the stuff they had bought and the bottles of drinks waiting to be put away he made a face. "Seems I needed to work overtime to pay for all that lot," he said, good-temperedly.

Leonie fed Samantha again while Paula got a meal ready. "I don't know what I'd have done without you today, Leonie," she said.

"I know why you asked me now," smirked Leonie.

"I wouldn't have believed a baby could make such a difference in a home," she said. "I seem to do nothing else but look after Samantha and if there's someone else to give her her bottle now and again it's marvellous."

"I've had very little time to help out," said Ron. "I've been busier than ever since we had the baby."

"That's because you're such a good accountant," said Paula, smiling at him, fondly.

After a meal and an hour of relaxation Ron was a different person. All his fatigue disappeared and he was full of life and vitality. Paula was good for him. She let him relax and didn't bother him about anything when he came home until he'd had a chance to unwind after a day's work.

During the evening there was a constant coming and going of friends. Leonie had never met a household like it. There always seemed to be someone arriving. "There's never a dull moment here," she said, to Paula.

"No. We're very lucky, we have lots of friends."

"And you make them welcome," said Leonie.

"Oh, I don't put myself out all that much," said Paula. "People have to take me as they find me."

"I think that's why they like to come. You don't make them feel you are put out by their visits."

"And I nearly always find them something to do," she said, laughing. "They can have anything they like to eat so long as they are willing to help in the preparation."

28

Leonie could see that was so. She had one buttering rolls, another preparing the salad, someone else was making coffee while she herself was filling *hors d'oeuvre* dishes. It seemed there would be quite a crowd staying for supper. Paula herself was doing nothing except tell them where to find everything.

Leonie had always been very fond of Paula. They had known each other through schooldays. Neither of them had wanted to go on to university. Leonie had taken a course in hairdressing and Paula had worked in an accountant's office and that was how she came to meet Ron, who had now started up on his own. And it was through Paula that Leonie had met Mark who had very little time to spare when she first met him for he had been studying in the evenings and working in industry in the daytime. When he had passed his examinations he had been given a good position and Leonie had expected he would go on from there, little realizing that he would be expected to do more studying in America for the benefit of his firm. How foolish she had been to resent his being sent away for his own benefit as well as the firm's. It was only because she had been so eagerly awaiting her wedding day and couldn't bear to think of it being put off.

Late in the evening Mark and his girl-friend Josy called in. Leonie was poring over a crossword puzzle with Ron's brother Steven and she was laughing over the stupid suggestions he was making for the missing words. She saw Mark glance her way but she pretended not to notice and decided to ignore him as he had ignored her the previous evening. But she managed to get a clear picture of his girl-friend. She was a quietly spoken girl, blonde and very pretty. She gave an appearance of being rather fragile, but spitefully Leonie told herself she probably wasn't half so fragile as she looked.

"If you want anything to eat," Paula said to them, "you'll have to help yourselves. I'm too shattered to look

29

after you."

"Well, we've been out for a meal," said Mark, "but if you've got anything very nice we might have some."

He went to the table where everything had been put out for people to help themselves and Leonie noticed how he turned to Josy, as if she was very special, asking her if she would like anything.

"I'd love a coffee," she said, looking up at him, intimately, and they both went off into the kitchen to get some.

Suddenly Leonie felt no longer interested in the crossword puzzle and she put the paper down. When Mark and Josy returned with their coffee she felt she had to get away. It was warm in the room and a pleasant evening so it gave her the opportunity to slip outside for a breath of air.

She went down the veranda steps and along the garden path, across the lawn to the end of the garden where it was possible to look out over the fields beyond. She watched the lights from cars as they made their way along the winding narrow lanes in the distance. Someone else had had the same idea as herself to get away from the warm atmosphere indoors and she could hear them chattering and giggling.

She felt very lonely. Lonelier than she'd ever done in her life. Dreadful jealousy rose within her as she thought of Josy with Mark. He was so attentive to her, reminding her of how he had once been with herself, but now he couldn't even be friendly for politeness sake. He either ignored her or was sarcastic.

Now that she had seen him with Josy she wished she could get away and that the christening was over. She strolled to the other side of the garden and out of the shadows a tall man approached her. She found herself caught up in his arms and held very close before his mouth came down upon hers. She knew without a doubt that it was Mark and she was too dumbfounded to respond at first. Why was he doing this to her? As he became more passionate she responded, clinging to him, and finding herself drowning in ecstasy. She had never been so carried away before, not even by Mark, and she clung to him wanting to hold on to him forever.

" Oh, Mark!" she gasped, when he released her.

" Why, it's you, Leonie!"

" Whoever did you think it was?"

" Well, that would be telling. I must say your technique has improved a great deal."

She was furious and lashed out at him. He had humiliated her and made her feel ashamed. " You, you hateful creature, you," she cried, trying to release her arm which he held in a firm grip.

" Now, now," he laughed. " You know you enjoyed it."

" I didn't know it was you," she lied. " Like you I thought it was someone else."

" So that was why you kissed me like that. Lucky fellow. Did you think it was Steve? You seem to have made quite a hit with him."

" Mind your own business," she said, and wondered how she could re-enter the house without anyone seeing her for her face was flushed and she was almost in tears with anger. " I'm sure Josy wouldn't be pleased to know you were out here kissing girls in the way you just kissed me," she said.

" Do you think my technique's improved?" he asked, and she could tell he was almost chuckling.

" I think you've been drinking."

" No more than I should," he said. " You should know that I've never over indulged."

" I don't know that I know you very well at all," she said. " Did you go round kissing other girls when you were engaged to me?"

" I'm not engaged to Josy, yet," he said. " I'm being very careful. You know what they say. ' Once bitten twice shy '. I want a wife who would be sensible enough to know that a man wouldn't go off on a training course without good reason."

" I hope you find someone who would be willing to put off her wedding without some protest, or if she did, that you'd be sensitive enough to know how she felt and be patient until she accepted that it was important for both of you that you went. You could try asking her if she would mind if you went instead of announcing with no warning that you were going."

He was about to say something when they heard Josy calling. " Mark is here, Josy," cried Leonie, and in a low voice to Mark she said, " She's welcome to you."

Her face had lost its high colour now and she was able to go indoors reasonably sure of herself. Steve had finished the crossword puzzle and he called her to see. " Send it off," he said. " You might win, and if you do, don't forget I helped you to do it."

" Right, we'll go fifty-fifty," she laughed, and was still managing to laugh and look as if she hadn't a care in the world when Mark came in from the garden with Josy.

The visitors began to leave and Leonie started to clear up after them. " I haven't the energy to do anything," said Paula. " I think I'll go off to bed and get up early in the morning. I have Mrs. Hackett coming in to help anyway. She comes in three mornings a week since I've had Samantha and she promised to come and help me tomorrow for the christening."

" You go on up," said Leonie. " I'll just finish putting this stuff away and then I'll be up too."

But once Paula and Ron had gone up to bed she made a good job of clearing everything away and leaving the place all spick and span. She wanted to tire herself out thoroughly so that she would sleep. She knew that as soon as she got to bed she would start thinking and her thoughts would be of Mark and that kiss in the garden. She had been in no doubt it was Mark from the beginning and something told her he had known it was her though he pretended he didn't. It was a dirty trick. She had been completely carried away and he'd

32

known. Perhaps that was his way of getting his revenge on her for letting him down in the past. He had enjoyed discovering that she was still vulnerable to his kisses.

She went off to bed telling herself that by this time tomorrow night she would be back in Cornwall and she would put all thoughts of Mark Trueman from her mind. Perhaps she would allow herself to fall in love with Justin Lewis. It wouldn't be too difficult.

Before going to sleep she made herself think of Justin instead of Mark. He had approached her when she took over her little gift shop with a view to allowing him to sit in her shop and sketch customers as they were meandering round. It could lead to orders for himself for portraits, or some might like to buy his sketches which he did spontaneously, and in any case it would bring people into her shop out of curiosity.

Leonie couldn't see any reason at all why she should object. He said he would seat himself in a corner, out of the way, and keep himself busy, and that he had done. It had been a tremendous boost for the shop. One or two portraits had been placed in the window. Justin didn't mind a group of people watching him at work. He was very considerate, and would never start immediately on another portrait when he'd finished one, but would allow a pause in between in order that people would look around the gift shop while they were waiting and this brought in good results for Leonie. He was an excellent portrait artist. She told him he should be doing far better than sitting in her little shop doing portraits, but he said he was happy working that way, and she had no complaints at all.

He had done numerous portraits of Leonie in slack moments and they had become great pals. He often helped her out when she was busy, packing up gifts and advising customers and they were both making a comfortable living. They had to make sufficient in the summer months to keep them through the winter when there were no tourists, but this they were quite able to do. Justin anyway, liked the wintertime to paint pictures of the sea when there was a storm, and landscapes while they were no people around. He had been successful in selling many of his pictures at a good price. He enjoyed his work and fame and fortune didn't bother him.

While Leonie was staying at Paula's her mother and her aunt had volunteered to look after her shop for her. They often gave her a hand and to them it was a pleasure. They didn't look on it as work at all but felt privileged to be called upon.

Lately Leonie had felt that Justin was becoming more than fond of her. Sometimes when her mother and aunt were helping out he had asked her to leave them to it for a short time and go out with him for a break. He had an old wreck of a car, but it got them about, and they went away from the busy coast with the masses of holidaymakers, and found pretty little villages inland.

Justin always had a sketch book with him and often he couldn't resist the temptation to sketch a lovely scene although he, like Leonie, was supposed to be taking a break from his work. " But I don't regard sketching and painting as work," he told Leonie. " It's my life. I live for capturing beautiful scenes and interesting faces," and she watched in fascination as he worked.

Out in the little villages they could get meals costing far less than in the holiday resorts and the places were more picturesque.

One day he had told her that he had never thought more of any girl than he did of her, and she had told him about Mark. It had been only fair to tell him that she had been in love and though her engagement was broken she hadn't stopped loving Mark.

" You shouldn't be spoiling your life over a man who doesn't care for you," he told her. " You say he's been back from America nearly a year and he's made no attempt to see you. What sort of man is that?"

" He's the man I love," said Leonie. " I know it's hopeless and I've got to get over him, but I can't at the moment. Sometimes I feel my love is so strong it must draw him to me. Why should I be made to love him as I do if he's not for me?"

" These things happen all the time," said Justin.

She had looked at the dark-eyed fellow with his thick black beard and dark curly hair. Why couldn't she love him as she loved Mark?

When she returned to her shop she would try to fall in love with Justin. She admired his work tremendously and felt proud to know such a clever artist who was famous in a small way. They talked of poor artists but Justin wasn't poor. He made quite a good living, but then he worked a good many hours. During the holiday season Leonie kept her gift shop open quite late in the evenings and Justin was always there taking orders for portraits until Leonie was ready to go.

Her mother liked Justin and had told Leonie that it was obvious that he was in love with her. "You don't think there's any chance of you and Mark making it up do you?" she asked.

" I don't know," said Leonie. "Perhaps if we saw each other. It was a mistake to come down here. I should have waited until he returned from America to see if he wanted to start where we left off before he went away."

" It's been nearly two years since you saw him, love. If he wanted you he would have put himself out to come and see you. Paula could have told him where you were if he wanted to know."

And then Paula had invited her to the christening and Leonie had accepted her invitation with hope in her heart. She was bound to meet Mark again and she prayed he wanted to see her as much as she wanted to see him.

She lay in bed thinking of that kiss once more. If only he

had been affected by it in the same way as she had been. She was sure now that he had wanted to hurt her. So why couldn't she stop thinking about him and concentrate on Justin, who was a far nicer fellow?

THREE

The day of the christening party was beautiful. The heat
wave which was being enjoyed all over the country showed
no signs of ending and so everyone was able to attend the
church ceremony wearing gay summer clothes.

Leonie wore a white dress with low elasticated neckline.
The bodice fitted her rounded figure perfectly. It was em-
broidered with a colourful motif. The waist was ruched and
the full skirt had a deep frilled hem. With the dress she
wore a large brimmed hat. Her arms and shoulders were
deeply tanned for she had spent a great deal of time on the
sea wall in Cornwall catching the sun. Her sandals had very
high heels so she looked tall and elegant.

She was not surprised to learn that Josy was to be
Samantha's other godmother, and Mark, of course, was to be
godfather. They set off for the church in several cars all
following each other like a convoy. " Have we got the
baby?" cried Mark, before getting into his car.

They set off for a picturesque little village church where
Mark and Paula had been christened. Paul's parents, Mr. and
Mrs. Trueman, had arrived early that morning, proudly
bringing along the christening robe in which their own son
and daughter had been christened. Samantha, for whom all
this was in aid of, slept peacefully. " I'll bet she'll yell the
place down while we're in church," said Paula, and she
certainly did. She objected to being disturbed.

Leonie had the honour of holding her as they stood around
the font and felt awfully embarrassed when Samantha
stretched and kicked and yelled in her arms, feeling in some

way she was responsible for her tantrum, and was not capable of comforting her. Seeing her flushed cheeks Mark smiled at her. " She'll be all right after the christening when the little devil inside her has been cast out."

Leonie had to laugh and she was pleased to know he had tried to make her feel at ease. And as if his words had come true, Samantha calmed down and was very good after the vicar handed her back to Leonie, when her baptism was over. Outside the church when cameras were busy clicking she looked most angelic.

Mrs. Trueman came to Leonie and told her how nice she looked in her large hat and pretty dress. " You are looking very well," she said.

Leonie liked Mark's mother and it was nice of her to come and be so civil to her knowing she had given up her son when he went to America.

Back at Paula's and Ron's the champagne flowed freely as they ' wet the baby's head ' so to speak. All the baby's gifts were set out for everyone to admire. Leonie had given her a silver goblet with her name inscribed in the pattern.

All the time Leonie felt her eyes straying to Mark who was looking marvellous in a light brown suit with a cream shirt. He seemed far more handsome now than when she'd been engaged to him and she had been stupid enough to let him go. She watched him with Josy and wondered if she would be the one to share his beautiful house with him. Somehow, to Leonie, she didn't seem his type at all and yet he was most attentive and charming to her. She couldn't imagine his ever being sarcastic to Josy. She would probably burst into tears if he was and he would be quick to comfort her, but Leonie retaliated by being just as rude or even more so in return.

Once she caught Mark looking at herself and for a moment she thought she caught a kind of longing expression in his eyes, but as soon as he knew she was aware that he was looking at her he turned away and began to talk to someone at his side.

Soon Leonie would have to start on her journey home, perhaps never to see Mark again, or if she did, he would be married. In a way she wanted to get the moment of parting over, and in another, she wanted to linger, feeling she couldn't take herself away without being at least on friendly terms with Mark. He had only spoken about half a dozen friendly sentences to her all the time she had been here.

She waylaid Paula at last and said, " I'll have to be on my way, Paula, it's a long journey back home."

" You must have something to eat before you go," her friend declared, and though Leonie protested that she wasn't hungry, she was drawn into the kitchen to have some of the food that would soon be set out for all the other guests.

" What's all this?" said Mark, coming into the kitchen and seeing Leonie perched on a breakfast stool with a plateful of food.

" Leonie has to leave soon," said Paula.

" You're not travelling all the way to Cornwall now?" he said, incredulously.

" I've told her she can stay. I don't mind how long she stays with me, I shall miss her, she's been so helpful to me while she's been here."

" The roads won't be so busy at this time in the day," said Leonie. " I'd rather travel on the motorways in the evening when there's not so much traffic about. Besides, I can't leave my mother in charge of my shop any longer."

" You don't mean to say your mother has taken up hairdressing?" said Mark.

Leonie laughed. " Good heavens, no," she said. " I'm not a hairdresser any more. I had to give it up. The chemicals didn't suit my hands and the doctor said I would have to find another way of earning my living."

" Oh," he said, thoughtfully. " That must have been a blow to you. You always wanted your own hairdressing salon."

39

" It couldn't be helped," she shrugged. " I bought a little gift shop on the sea front and it's doing quite well."

" It's a long journey for you to take all on your own," he said, and she was sure he looked concerned.

" I came on my own," she said, " I can go back on my own."

Shortly afterwards she called ' good-bye ' to everyone and one or two special friends came to see her on her way including Paula and her mother, and Mark and Josy. For a moment or two she found herself looking into Mark's eyes and he seemed to hold hers with his keen blue ones. It was almost as if he was questioning her, but it was too late for any talk now, she gave what she hoped was a cheerful wave, and started on the long journey home.

She found before she got very far that the tears were streaming down her cheeks so badly she just had to stop and gain control of herself. She spread her map on the seat beside her and made an attempt to study it. She wasn't very sure about her way back and she had got to concentrate on the journey. With an effort she choked back her sobs, decided which was the best route to take to get on the motorway, and then she started the car again.

Mile after mile sped by. She wasn't a dare-devil driver, but neither was she a slow one, and her car swallowed up the miles on the comparatively quiet M5 leading to the south. The time seemed to go as quickly as the miles were covered. She stopped for a rest at eight o'clock at one of the service stations and had a coffee. It had done her good to have to concentrate on her driving for she was no longer near to tears and when she went to the ladies she examined her eyes for signs of tears and saw there were no signs left. She didn't want her mother and her aunt to feel concerned about her when they saw her, though she expected they would be in bed by the time she got home.

She moved on to the A38 through Somerset, left Glaston-bury behind, then Taunton, travelled on to Honiton and

40

Exeter. She was beginning to feel very tired and sang to herself as she drove to keep herself alert. It would have been better to have someone with her to talk to her and keep her wide awake. She took another break before the pubs closed and managed to find one that provided snacks and she took a good rest before setting off on the last lap of the journey. It was very dark as she drove down the final unlit narrow lanes to her aunt's bungalow. It had been a pleasant journey, no rain, a glorious sunset, no traffic jams. The beautiful scenery and concentration on her driving had taken her mind off her sorrow over leaving Mark, perhaps never to see him again. She would have to get over him. She hadn't really expected anything to come of her visit to his sister, but there had been a slight hope, now she had none.

It was in the early hours of the morning that she arrived home tired and weary. She let herself in quietly, made herself a coffee and then went quietly to bed, but her mother was awake. She called, " That you, Leonie? Everything okay?"

" Yes, Mum," said Leonie, whispering so as not to wake her aunt.

" We're both awake," said her mother. " We couldn't get off to sleep until we knew you were back safe and sound."

Leonie smiled as she went into her own room after calling good night to them both. She was not surprised that they had been concerned for her. They would have been terribly worried if she had not come back tonight. She couldn't have phoned them for they were not on the phone to let them know she was staying overnight.

Thankfully she lay back on her pillows and closed her eyes only to feel herself still travelling along winding roads and country lanes. It had been a long journey, she was very tired, but sleep didn't come for a long time, for she was over tired and couldn't relax after the hours of concentrated driving. She found the tears slipping down her face again as she thought of Mark. She thought she had shed all the tears she would over him, but seeing him again had made her realize how much she had loved and wanted him even though it had been so long since she saw him.

The following morning when it seemed she had only just slipped into sleep she found a hand on her shoulder and opening her eyes saw her mother with a cup of tea for her. "What time is it?" she asked, irritably.

"Don't worry, you needn't get up. Your aunt and I are going to the shop for you and you can sleep on for a bit. I've put a casserole in the oven so you can have some before you come to the shop and leave some for us two."

"Sure you don't mind going to the shop, Mum?" said Leonie, struggling up and taking the tea from her, and feeling ashamed of her irritability.

"No, we love it," said her mother. "We've taken a lot of money for you over the week-end. Justin has been a big help to us."

"Good," said Leonie, but at the moment she couldn't care less about money or anything else she was just dying to get back to sleep.

It was eleven-thirty when she awoke again and she could smell the casserole cooking and realized she was hungry. By the time she had taken a shower and dressed ready for the shop it was getting on for twelve so she decided to have an early lunch and go. She couldn't resist the delicious smell of cooking any longer. The meat was beautifully tender and she thoroughly enjoyed her heaped plateful of mixed vegetables and steak.

Soon she was walking towards her shop in the bright sunshine wearing a red spotted dress with shoulder straps. It was no use taking her car anywhere near the sea front for she would not find a parking space anywhere at this time in the year.

She had soft flat-heeled sandals on her feet for comfort as she would be standing a good many hours. She enjoyed her gift shop, on the whole, but this morning she couldn't see

42

any point in working or anything else. Life was completely meaningless if you couldn't be with the one you loved.

Justin, her mother and her aunt were so pleased to see her when she arrived at the shop that she felt a little ashamed of her earlier depression, for here were three people who loved her and she owed it to them to be happy.

When the older women had gone leaving her alone with Justin he came over to her when he had finished the portrait he was doing and asked her how the christening party had gone.

"It was a beautiful week-end," she said, not meeting his eyes.

"And Mark, did you see him?"

She looked up at Justin then, seeing that his dark hair seemed even longer and curlier than ever and his dark beard was thick and black. "Yes, I did, Justin, and it was no good. He's planning to get married soon. He's had a house built, and he told me it was ready for his wife."

"And he didn't want to mend your broken engagement?"

"No. He seemed to despise me at times."

"I don't believe anyone could despise you, princess," he said. "You said he told you you could have your ring back any time you liked. Why didn't you ask him for it? Tell him how you felt?"

"Oh, I couldn't do that," she said. "I might have done if he'd shown any signs of wanting me to ask him for it, but he didn't."

"It wouldn't have done any harm to confess that you deeply regretted giving it back to him."

"I would have felt so humiliated if he'd told me he didn't want me any more, which I'm sure is the way he feels."

Justin gave a deep sigh. "You girls are all alike. You expect a man to take the initiative every time. How many times have girls humiliated men by rejecting their love? Men have to learn to take it you know."

" It's the way girls are made," she smiled. " We don't like a man to think we're running after him. We expect them to do the running."

" Well, I'll come running for you any time you like, princess," he said, " and if you wanted me I hope you'd be sensible enough to tell me, and not be afraid of losing your pride in admitting you loved me."

" I wish I did love you, Justin," she said.

" So do I," he sighed. " Still we've plenty of time," he grinned. " We're both young."

Leonie went down the narrow corridor and down the steps into the kitchen below to make some coffee and called to Justin to serve her customers while she was away. When she had her own coffee she went back into the shop and Justin took his sandwiches down into the kitchen to eat while he drank the coffee she had left for him.

" We're almost like a married couple," Leonie told herself, as she watched him go down into the kitchen. She liked him a lot and he loved her. Perhaps she was being silly in not putting Mark out of her mind. She thought of Paula with her little baby and knew how much she envied her.

How Leonie would have loved a baby like Samantha. She tried to picture herself married to Justin and having a family, but just couldn't imagine married life with him. They wouldn't have a home like Paula had she didn't suppose. Not that she wanted anything so grand as Paula's, she would be satisfied with much less, but would Justin be in a position to buy a house for her? Would he want to? At the moment he was sharing a fisherman's cottage with a couple of other fellows, both artists like himself. " Artists don't live like other people," she told herself. She couldn't imagine Justin at all in an ordinary house, and yet she knew he was making good money with his portraits alone, but he spent all his time sketching. It wouldn't be much of a life for his wife, she thought, and then she realized that again she was expecting a man to put herself before his work. Justin loved sketch-

44

ing. He said it wasn't like work to him, yet she had been wondering if he would be prepared to get himself a job with regular hours if he married.

"Did you meet the girl Mark is to marry?" asked Justin, making her start. She had been so far away she hadn't heard him come back into the shop.

"I don't know," she said. "He was with a very pretty girl named Josy and he seemed to think a great deal of her, but his sister says he is quite fond of his secretary and she isn't sure which one he intends to marry."

"Perhaps he doesn't want either of them," said Justin. "There's nothing to stop him getting married if he's had a house built all ready for his bride, so what's stopping him from fixing a date? Perhaps he too, is pining for you."

"He couldn't be, could he?" she said. "He would have sought me out and asked me to make it up with him if he felt like that."

Leonie went on to tell him about the lovely home Paula had. "Her husband is an accountant and must be making lots of money for they live extremely well," she said.

"I could buy you a nice home, princess," he said, as if he had been reading her thoughts while he had been down in the kitchen. "I worked for a good many years in my father's business. He wouldn't hear of me becoming an artist. Had no time for idlers, he told me. Anyway, I was fond of my dad and knew he was lonely when my mother died. If I'd left him to live as I live now he would have been heart-broken so I stayed with him. When he died I sold up the business and came down here. I don't rely on the money I earn now, I'm not hard up. I could give you a home as good as Paula's I daresay."

"Oh, Justin," she said. "I'm glad you aren't a poverty-stricken artist, but if I loved you it wouldn't matter if you were. I'd want to marry you and live the sort of life you want to live."

"Well," he paused. "I just thought I'd let you know all

45

the same that I would consider changing my way of life for you, and that I could change it quite easily." He fingered his beard, lovingly. " I'd get rid of this too, and get my hair cut," he grinned.

Leonie laughed gaily, and impulsively she lifted her face and gave him a kiss. " Dear Justin," she said. " I wouldn't allow you to change your whole way of life for my sake."

He caught her close and gave her a kiss. " I love you, Leonie, I'd do anything for you. When you allowed me to come and make use of your shop you probably thought I was a down and out and yet you were prepared to help me."

" I never thought of you as a down and out," she protested. " There was something about you that told me you were not a hippy type, and I do like you, beard and all."

Laughing he held her close and she buried her face against his chest. As he held her in his arms it was as if she was transported back to the garden at Paula's when Mark held her in his arms. She suddenly put her hands to her face and he knew she was crying.

" I know, love," he said, holding her comfortingly. " I wish you could forget him."

The slight respite they had had in the shop while most of the holidaymakers had been having their midday meal ended and the shop began to fill up with people having a look round or buying gifts to take home for their friends. Leonie was kept busy wrapping necklaces made with sea shells, more expensive necklaces, bracelets, pictures, leather goods, stationery sets, pottery made in Cornwall, and goods of all descriptions suitable for presents.

Leonie particularly loved helping little children to choose presents for their school friends, or grannie and grandpa. They always took a long time to make up their minds, but she had infinite patience with them.

Sometimes Justin would make a quick sketch of youngsters and hand them the sketch free of charge which delighted them, and he didn't lose by being generous with his sketches because it often led to parents coming along to see the man who did such sketches and they often decided to have a 'proper' one done, when they discovered what a clever artist he was.

Since her little talk with Justin, Leonie felt closer to him than she'd ever done before, but she didn't kid herself she had fallen in love with him. It seemed he felt that there was a change in their relationship and he asked her to let him take her out for a meal when they closed the shop.

"Yes, I'd like that, Justin," she said, and they closed the shop a little earlier than usual so that she could go home and change. She decided to wear the dress she had worn for the christening. She knew Justin would appreciate it.

When her mother saw her all ready to go out she said, "Darling, you look lovely. Did Mark see you in that dress?"

"He did," said Leonie, "but it didn't bring him to my feet."

"I should think you'll forget all about him then. If he couldn't be swept away seeing you like that, so lovely, he never will."

When Justin arrived he took her hand and held her away from him, so that he could study her better. "Well, you look absolutely fine, a real princess," he said. "Everyone's going to envy me tonight."

In the past when Justin took her out it had worried her when he spent his money on her in case it was more than he could afford, but now she knew she need not have bothered. Justin was, perhaps, better off than Mark, and just as clever, though there might have been many people who had looked at his long hair, thick beard, and the clothes he wore, mostly jeans and a check shirt, and classed him as a lay-about which he said she probably thought he was. But she had recognized from the first moment she saw him that he wasn't a ne'er do well. She had sensed his integrity from the beginning when he had asked her politely if he could use her shop for sketching in, which he believed would be to their mutual

47

advantage, and it had been. He had drawn people in, and she had sold far more gifts than she had done before.

As usual he took her away from the coastal area into a small village where he knew a first-class hotel and had booked a table. He was looking very smart in a dark suit and white shirt. It was very rarely that she saw him dressed so formally. She saw that eyes turned as they went to their table. Justin was a very handsome young man and she knew the girls envied her. What she didn't realize was that she also was drawing many admiring glances from both men and women for she was really very attractive.

Justin went out of his way to cheer her up. He told her of the mischievous tricks he had got up to as a child having her in fits of laughter. Then he told her of the different girls he had been with.

" I nearly landed myself with one of them for life," he smiled. " Her name was Doreen. We actually got engaged and yet the more I got to know her the less I wanted to be tied to her for life."

" How did you get rid of her?" laughed Leonie.

" I grew this," he said, his eyes twinkling as he fondled his beard. " I didn't realize it would bring the break between me and Doreen, but it did. She was furious with me and said if I didn't get rid of it she was finished with me. Well, I didn't get rid of it, and she did finish with me. I couldn't believe my luck," he chuckled.

Leonie laughed. " That was less reason for breaking her engagement than mine. Fancy breaking it off with your fellow just because he grew a beard."

" Some girls don't like a beard," he said seriously. " If it had been anyone but Doreen I might have got rid of it. I would for you for instance."

" But I haven't said I don't like it," she laughed, pro-testingly. " I couldn't imagine you without it. It's part of your personality."

He reached for his wallet and drew out a picture of him-

48

self with his hair cut reasonably short and he was clean-shaven. "There, can you believe that was me?"

She studied it carefully and then looked at him. "I would never have recognized you," she said. "You look an entirely different person there."

"I was," he said. "I was, according to my father, earning my living in a respectable fashion. If he knew how I lived now he would never believe it. It would shock him to death," and then he smiled, realizing what he had said. His father was already dead.

"I suppose it must be awful to have neither a father nor a mother alive," she said. "I do have my mother and it's nice to feel you belong to someone."

"Loneliness doesn't bother me," said Justin. "I like to feel free. Don't get me wrong. I loved my parents but I can live my own life quite happily. There are no restrictions upon me. I can live as I choose."

Leonie looked at him, thoughtfully. She believed that Justin was one of those men who are entirely self-sufficient. He lived for his art, and anything that interfered with that would be soul-destroying to him. He had told her he loved her, but if she returned his love what sort of life would she have? She would have to come second to his art, for he would devote most of his time to it. Perhaps that was why men like Justin were often inclined to take their love where they found it and didn't get tied up permanently with a woman. She didn't know all that much about Justin, but from what he'd been telling her tonight he had known plenty of girls. He hadn't been bragging, just trying to amuse her.

"You are very serious," he said. "Come on, drink up your wine and let me refill your glass."

She smiled. "We've already got through one bottle of wine and nearly this second one. Do you want to get me drunk?"

He laughed. "Have you ever been drunk?"

49

"No, I'm afraid to drink too much in case I become alcoholic and I'd be terrified to take drugs, and I've never smoked because I know it's a habit that's not easily broken once you've started. I don't take any risks, do I?"

"I've never smoked," he said. "I suppose that's because I've always got a piece of charcoal or a paint brush in my hand and if I'm bored instead of lighting up a cigarette I start sketching. I'm addicted to sketching, I suppose you might say. I can't say I haven't been drunk once or twice, but I seem to be able to consume alcohol without it having much effect on me. Or perhaps I've been stupidly drunk and haven't realized it. As for drug taking, I've never been tempted."

He went on to tell her about a friend of his who became a drug addict and finally took an overdose. "It broke his parents' hearts," he said. "He was their only son, and quite brilliant at school. He was given drugs when he was in his early teens, that's when the pushers like to get them, and they're addicts in no time."

"I suppose his parents didn't discover he was taking them until it was too late?"

"No, they didn't. That's the danger. When the effects start to show it's usually too late to help. By then they don't want to be helped. They don't want to be deprived of the drug and they don't care that it's destroying them."

He filled her glass for her. "Come, we're not going to be morbid," he said. "I brought you out to cheer you up."

"Well you have, Justin, I'm very grateful."

When they left the hotel she said, "I suppose I'm as near drunk tonight as I'll ever be. That wine has gone to my head, Justin, I feel quite woozy."

He laughed and put his arm around her. "Just to steady you," he grinned.

They went off to the car pretending to be very unsteady on their feet and when they reached the car Justin held her tighter and gave her a kiss. Just a very ordinary one and

50

Leonie felt so much in need of love she nearly pulled him closer to kiss him more passionately, but managed to draw away, telling herself she had certainly drunk more than she should have done. It wouldn't be fair to lead him on when she didn't want to be serious with him, or anyone for that matter.

Perhaps Justin sensed that his kiss didn't carry her away, making her long for him to follow up with kisses more emotional, expressing his love, for he was rather quiet on the journey back home. For the life of her Leonie couldn't make conversation, either, and suspected the wine had made her drowsy. All she wanted was to get home and into her bed to sleep and forget everything.

When they arrived at the bungalow he took her hand in his for a moment or two, gently stroking the back of it. "You have lovely soft hands, do you know that?" he said.

"I know they weren't tough enough to stand the chemical we used in hairdressing," she said.

"I'm glad," he told her. "If you'd been able to keep your hairdressing business we should never have met, should we?"

"I suppose not. Although I might have come down this way with mum. She wanted to come and keep her sister company."

"Do you think it was fate intending us to meet?"

"Perhaps," said Leonie.

He didn't attempt to kiss her again and as she went indoors after thanking him for a lovely evening, she wondered if fate had brought her this way, and whether she would fall in love with Justin given time.

FOUR

After the heat-wave which had lasted several weeks there came thunderstorms and torrential rain. This in no way affected the trade in Leonie's gift shop, in fact she was busier than ever, for holidaymakers, searching for shelter from the rain, wandered round the gift shops, and there was the added attraction in Leonie's shop of Justin and his artistic talent. He did a roaring trade as one after another decided to have a portrait of themselves done to pass the time away out of the rain.

He wanted to pay Leonie extra because he was making extra money, but she refused to take more than they'd agreed upon in the beginning. But Justin was very generous and brought her gifts to show his gratitude. He bought her tapes of her favourite music which was his favourite too. He took her out for meals and refused to let her pay her whack. And, what Leonie appreciated more than anything, was the fact that he did her book-keeping for her. Leonie was no good at all at keeping accounts, and there was such a lot to do keeping shop accounts for the income tax authorities, showing value added tax and so forth which Leonie hated.

She could see that her profits were soaring. They'd had an extremely good summer. " If I make money at this rate I shall be able to retire at an early age," she told Justin.

" I could retire now if I wanted," said Justin. " Let's, shall we? I'd take you all over the world."

" That would be lovely," said Leonie. " I may take you up on that one day."

" Soon," he said, coaxingly, putting his arm across her

52

shoulder. " We could have a fine time together."

" Well, we're together all day now," she said, " and for the moment we'll leave it at that."

Since she had met Mark again and nothing had come of it Justin was more hopeful that Leonie would turn to him. He knew there was no one else in her life and he began to treat her as his girl. Leonie told him it was his own fault if he got hurt for she promised him nothing. " I'm glad of your company, Justin. In fact I don't know what I'd do without you, but that doesn't mean I'm in love with you."

" I can wait," he said. " I'm a very patient man."

He reminded her that if she did decide she would like to marry him he would buy her a home and they would settle down to ordinary domesticity.

" You would be bored to tears in no time," she told him.

" I wouldn't, not with you, Leonie."

" But you're as happy as the day is long doing portraits of people and joining in the holiday spirit with them."

" Well, yes, I am, but I wouldn't have to give up sketching and painting when we're married, not completely, would I?"

" You couldn't, you know that," she laughed. " I'd come second to your work, always."

" You would be as important as my work," he said, seriously, " and I love my work very much, so that's how much I love you."

Once he suggested they got married and carried on living just as they were for the time being.

" We're happy as we are," she said, " I don't see why we have to be married."

" Don't you?" he asked, quizzically. " Wouldn't you like to be with me at night as well as all day?"

" No," she said, ignoring the cheeky look in his eyes. " We should probably get fed up with each other very quickly if we didn't have a break from each other at the end of every day."

53

" Oh, Leonie, my love, how can you say that? The night times would be the best."

" I wouldn't know about that," she said. " I've never spent the night with a member of the opposite sex. You've had more experience than I have."

" I can recommend it," he smirked. " It's far better to share your bed than to sleep alone."

Although Justin teased her and tried to persuade her into marriage he didn't pester her and try to force her into doing something she was extremely doubtful about. He valued her friendship too much to jeopardize it by being a too persistent lover.

Leonie's stock was becoming sadly depleted after the enormous amount of trade she had done during the summer and she decided she ought to go and visit the warehouses and buy in some more. Even if she over bought it wouldn't matter because prices were increasing all the time so that any stock that didn't sell this year would be worth more by next.

" Would you mind running the shop for me for a whole day, Mum?" she asked. " I know auntie will keep you company."

" Oh, I love it," said her Aunt Louise. " If you ever thought of giving up your shop I'd love to buy it from you. I feel so happy after I've spent a few hours in the shop serving people and trying to help them make up their minds."

" You might find it would be too much for you if you had to work the number of hours I do," said Leonie.

" We managed while you were away for the christening," said her mother. " We aren't doddering old women yet you know."

" Indeed you aren't," said Leonie, " and if you both love the shop so much I'll certainly keep you in mind when I decide to sell up."

" Have you had any such thoughts?" asked her mother.

" Not seriously. Justin keeps hinting he'd like us to be

married, and he says he would buy a house for me. If I accepted I would like to have more freedom, the shop takes up all my time during the season, and then, I'd like a family."

Her mother's face lit up. " Oh, Leonie, I'd be so happy for you. Justin is very nice, and you know I'd love grand-children."

" Wouldn't Justin want to go on with his portraits after you were married?" asked Aunt Louise. " How would he earn a living if he didn't do that?"

" He's independent without working in the shop. I expect he would carry on with his art, and when he has time to paint he is successful with his landscape pictures, and sea views."

Leonie knew her mother and aunt liked the shop and she was often very glad of their help. Stock had to be put away, or put on display and there was the tedious job of putting price tags on everything, in addition to serving customers and they didn't make a fuss about the less pleasant jobs as some younger assistants might have done. It gave them both something to live for feeling they were useful in some way apart from just in the home.

When she told Justin she was going out for the day to do some buying in he immediately offered to accompany her.

" Don't be silly," she said. " You can't lose a day's work."

" Who can't?" he said. " I'm my own boss, remember. I can give myself a day off whenever I want to."

" I can't say I wouldn't be pleased to have company while I'm on my buying spree," she said, and immediately Justin put away his sketching block and was ready to go with her.

She had made a list of the items she was short of and added to it as Justin drove her to the warehouses, for he insisted on going in his car. The days were getting a little chillier now and Leonie was wearing a short jacket over her summer dress.

At the warehouse Justin went round with her helping her

55

to choose new stock. He came upon some beautiful silver-ware and cut-glass items and suggested she bought some.

" But it's terribly expensive, Justin," she said. " Do you think I would sell that sort of thing in my shop?"

" Your husband is right, madam," said the assistant. " You should try out some of our more expensive gifts. There are always people looking for something special."

Justin caught her eye as the assistant referred to him as her husband and she began to giggle, and his eyes were twinkling.

" We could always use them ourselves, darling, if they didn't sell," he said.

Smiling she allowed herself to be persuaded. She'd had a good year and didn't mind launching out a bit. But when she saw the amount she owed when she was presented with the bill she looked up at Justin with a grimace.

" I'll help you pay for it," he whispered.

" No you won't," she retorted.

" Well if you don't sell those expensive items I'll buy them from you."

" I'm not really worried," she assured him. " It's just that the bill it more than I'm used to. You've encouraged me to be extravagant."

" Not unwisely, I'm sure," he said. " Your shop attracts all sorts of people and you need to cater for everyone."

They left the warehouse and Leonie said she had to visit another one as they couldn't get all her requirements from one place. They stopped for a meal before going on, and went for a walk round the small town. Justin took her hand as they strolled around. " How does it feel to have me as your husband?" he grinned, and she knew he was referring to the assistant mistaking him for her husband.

She didn't answer and he said, " We must look suited to each other or we wouldn't have been taken for husband and wife."

She smiled up at him. He was very nice and she could do

much worse than marry him.

On the way home he said, " How would you like to go to a dinner dance tonight?"

" I should love it," she said. " Mark and I used to go dancing a lot and I haven't been to any dances down here."

" I'll get the tickets," he said. " We'll try and get away a little earlier than usual."

They returned to find her mother and aunt had had a busy day in the shop and were glad when Justin offered to run them back to the bungalow. " We've had a very good day, indeed," said her Aunt Louise, excitedly. " We sold one of those mirrors with flowers on it, a child's wheelbarrow, and lots and lots of small gifts. I wouldn't have believed it so late in the year."

" I shall have to increase your salaries," laughed Leonie, who did pay them for services rendered, though they would have done it for love.

" Anyone enquire after me?" asked Justin.

" Yes, I told them you'd be back later as you told me to," said Mrs. Drew.

" Let's hope they don't keep me too late," he grinned, looking at Leonie. " We're going to a dance tonight."

" Lucky you," said Leonie's mum. " I used to love dancing when I was young."

" Who says you're not young still?" said Justin, putting his arms around her and swinging her round the shop while she screamed for him to let go. " Why you're as light as a feather," he said. " You should continue to go dancing to keep you young and fit."

He took Mrs. Drew and her sister off home and Leonie began to study the bills for all the stock she had bought. She had the job of working out all the retail prices and all the prices would have to be marked on the goods when Justin came back and unloaded the stock from his car for her. She was kept on her toes for people were coming in and out of the shop all the time and if they were not buying it was

57

necessary to watch out for shoplifters.

When Justin returned he brought in all her new stock, helped her to unwrap it and said he would help her put it away after he'd made some coffee for both of them. "I got the tickets while I was out," he said.

"Oh, did you?" She glanced at her watch. "Yes, of course, it wouldn't have taken you that long to take mum and auntie home."

"I had a job to get through the traffic," he said. "Did you miss me while I was gone?" he grinned, coming behind her and putting his arms round her waist.

"No, I didn't," she laughed. "I've been too busy."

He went off to make the coffee and produced some buns which he buttered. They always kept a stock of milk and sugar and butter in the kitchen downstairs.

"You're only having a couple of buns for now," he said. "You've got to keep yourself hungry for that lovely meal we're going to have tonight."

"It's you who has to watch your waistline," she retorted. "Not me. Just look at the size of you."

"I'm not fat," he protested.

"Nor thin," she said, dryly.

"Well I'll dance myself slim tonight," he said. "I'm looking forward to it, are you?"

"Yes," she said. "I think it's time I started to enjoy myself."

"That will be better than moping around."

"I haven't been moping around. I've been too busy to mope since I bought this shop."

"Would it be a great effort to give it up?"

"I don't know. I just look on it as a way of making a living. A very pleasant way, but it leaves little time for anything else in the holiday season. I would like to close at a respectable hour, but all the shops keep open late and I feel I have to. Besides people like to walk round the shops in the evening when it's too cold to sit on the beaches."

People who been hanging about waiting for Justin to do their portrait began to arrive and he was kept busy while Leonie tried to unpack her stock, put the price tags on in between serving her customers.

It was later than they intended when they left the shop at last. " I'll run you home," said Justin, " to save time." He had managed to park his car nearby which was not always possible in the summer.

" Wear that white dress you wore the other night," he said. " You look beautiful in that."

" Don't I look beautiful always?" she asked, coyly.

" You know you do, you minx," he said, giving her bottom a smack before getting into his car.

Happily Leonie got ready. " It's a good thing I have your auntie for company," said her mother, smiling. " We don't see much of you these days."

" The shop swallows up most of my time," she said. " Look at the time now, hardly worth going out, is it?"

Justin returned having made a quick change into an evening suit. " You look very handsome," she told him.

He grinned as he helped to put her white shawl around her shoulders. " You need that," he said. " It's gone quite cool."

" I'm just about dying of hunger," she said, as she sat beside him in the car. " Do we have to go very far?"

" Only a mile or two, I'll step on it," he said, " I'm ready to eat too," and soon he was speeding away down country lanes to the place he had chosen.

When they arrived, she ran into the dining-room of the large hotel when she left the car as a biting wind was blowing up. The warmth and luxury of the hotel was very welcoming: she waited for Justin to join her and then they were shown to their table. By now he was used to her likes and dislikes and she allowed him to order for her. The dining-tables were set at one end of the large room, and the other side was cleared for dancing and couples were already dancing on the polished dance floor while others, like themselves, were still dining.

It was a very pleasing atmosphere. They had had a busy day and were content to sit leisurely over their meal and watch the other dancers before getting up to dance themselves. And then Leonie discovered that Justin was a very good dancer. He led her perfectly and she followed his steps with ease. She hated to dance with a partner who kept her guessing what his next steps would be.

The lights were dim and it was very romantic. Justin was holding her very close and she saw that he had a dreamy look in his eyes. Was it due to the wine they had consumed? She smiled. He really was a dear. What would she do without him now?

They danced on and on until the early hours of the morning. Leonie hadn't enjoyed herself so much for ages. But all good things come to an end and at last it was time for her to collect her shawl and was ready for home.

They travelled home in companionable silence, both too tired to talk. The bungalow was in darkness of course when they arrived home for Leonie's mother and her aunt were in bed. "Would you like to come in for a coffee?" she asked Justin.

"I don't really want a coffee," he said. "But I'll come in with you. I don't want to leave you tonight, princess."

She laughed softly as they went indoors and when she switched the light on in the kitchen he switched it off again and drew her into his arms. The shawl slipped from her shoulders and he kissed her as he'd never done before. She didn't mind a kiss, he deserved that for being so good to her. His kisses travelled down her neck to her shoulder and still she didn't object. Her elasticated neckline made it easy for him to make her dress into an off the shoulder one, and his kisses were becoming far more passionate, and he was becoming more and more daring.

"No, no, Justin," she said, as his hands went exploring

lower and she felt the warmth of them. She had no wish to hurt him, she liked him so much, but he was going too far. He took no heed of her protests and she found his mouth going lower too. Tears began to stream down her face. If she loved him as he wanted her to she wouldn't have minded the liberties he was taking, but his actions told her all too clearly that liking a person is not loving. He lifted his lips to her mouth and tasted the salt tears. " Leonie!" he said, shocked, " You're crying."

That set her off into a storm of weeping and he immediately released her. " Leonie, don't," he said, in alarm. " I'm sorry. Really, I'm sorry. I shouldn't have."

But Leonie was not crying because he had made such passionate love to her, it was because she hadn't been able to respond in the way he wanted her to. She was crying because she didn't love him.

She had made him feel dreadful and she was sorry. " Justin," she wept. " I like you honestly. I didn't want to

" No I don't," he said. " I understand. I'm not the one make you feel awful. You must think I'm an awful prude." for you, and I wouldn't have admired you if you'd let me go on knowing that you didn't care for me that way. Don't cry, your mother will hear."

She gulped and he gave her his handkerchief to dry her eyes. She handed it back after drying her eyes. They had not switched on the light and she was thankful they didn't have to see each other's expression.

" Are you all right?" he asked, anxiously.

" Yes, Justin, I'm sorry."

" That's all right. I should be sorry. I think I'd better go. Good night, Leonie."

She went with him to the door and he took her hand before he went, giving it a friendly squeeze. " I guess I'm a stupid idiot," he said, and quickly got in his car and drove away.

After he'd gone Leonie couldn't stop crying. She had just

hurt Justin and he was the last person in the world she wanted to hurt. She hoped she hadn't made him feel ashamed of himself. After all, he had told her he loved her: he hadn't treated her that way because he had no respect for her. If she had loved him she would have had to stop him losing complete control of himself for she did not believe in pre-marital sex, but she felt she had humiliated him.

She went to bed feeling that something dreadful had happened. It was such a shame after such a wonderful day she and Justin had just spent together.

She got up the next day feeling dreadfully unhappy. She felt she didn't want to go to the shop. If Justin came she would feel embarrassed and if he didn't she would feel a great sense of loss. The shop would not be the same if Justin stayed away.

Fortunately, neither her mother nor her aunt noticed her listlessness before she set off after breakfast. She had only had a cup of coffee, feeling that food would choke her. Justin never arrived as early as she did and she let herself into the shop and tried to busy herself by carrying on where she had left off the previous day, pricing the remainder of the stock and putting it away.

Justin didn't come at his usual time and the morning dragged on until nearly midday. It seemed he wasn't going to come. Supposing she never saw him again. She felt really ill. Why couldn't two people of the opposite sex remain friends and not have the complication of falling in love? She knew she was not being logical. Friendship came before that special love that grew between a man and a woman. She had not fallen in love with Mark immediately. They had been good friends and then they realized they were in love. When Mark became passionate in his love-making it had been heavenly. She had never let him go too far but the temptation had been very strong.

She wondered if she would ever fall in love again. She didn't want to remain single all her life, but supposing she never fell in love again. That meant if she wanted to marry she would have to marry someone she didn't love, and why not Justin? He loved her. Could she pretend she loved him?

Or had she driven him away for good? Would he show his face again after the way she had behaved last night? She had been such a baby. She should have firmly told him there was nothing doing instead of letting him go on kissing her and then crying like a baby. What must he think of her?

It was almost one o'clock when he came into the shop. Their eyes met and she saw there was no condemnation in his. He just looked thoroughly miserable. He handed her a huge box of chocolates and she said, " Oh, Justin, you shouldn't have," and she reached up to give him a kiss.

" You shouldn't do that," he said. " You don't know what you do to me. Am I forgiven?"

" Justin, there's nothing to forgive."

" Sure?"

" I'm sure. I've been so miserable since you left me. I wouldn't upset you for the world."

" And I wouldn't hurt you, princess. We're still friends?"

" Of course. I should miss you dreadfully if you stopped coming."

He began to help her in the shop as he waited for clients to come to him. He was unusually reserved and Leonie felt that something between them was spoilt. They would never be quite the same again. Was it fair for her to expect Justin to keep coming to the shop when she had no love to offer him? She wanted to make things right between them and after a time she said, " Justin, you wouldn't want to marry me now you know I'm fond of you and not in love, would you?"

He turned to look at her incredulously. " Are you proposing to me?" he asked.

" I don't know," she said. " I've been thinking about us such a lot. I should miss you dreadfully if I never saw you again. All morning I've been completely wretched because you didn't come. I couldn't bear to think I'd upset you so much you wouldn't want to be bothered with me any more. I want to get married, Justin, but I'm afraid I may not be able to love anyone else as I loved Mark."

"You will," he said. He put his arm around her. "I would love to accept your proposal, Leonie, but I'm not going to, for the time being at least. I can wait. I rushed you, didn't I? If I was selfish I'd agree to our marriage right away, but I'm thinking of you, not myself. When you can tell me you are absolutely sure you want to marry me then I'll be on top of the world."

He held her close for a time and then released her. "Come on, cheer up, love. Your happiness is more important to me than anything. Always remember that."

A family came in. The parents wanted sketches of their children and Justin was kept busy for a long time. It was a good order for him and Leonie was glad because she felt he had wasted his morning because of her.

She had put out her expensive gifts on show in a special display hoping that she had not made a mistake in buying them. They looked very classy and, as Justin said, if they didn't sell they could have them for themselves. She knew her mother would be delighted with the cut-glass *hors d'oeuvre* dish, or the cut-glass fruit dish. While she was admiring them in contrast with her cheaper, sometimes trashy gifts, a middle-aged man came in and began inspecting them thoroughly. He seemed particularly interested in some silver-plated goblets of very good quality in a gift case. When he asked the price Leonie expected him to walk away, but instead he considered for a moment and then with a smile he said he would take them. "It's our silver wedding this year," he confided. "I want them for my wife."

Leonie looked towards Justin who was busily sketching to see if he had observed the sale of one of the expensive gifts he had persuaded her to buy. He had and she caught a humorous smile on his face as he continued with his sketching.

The man went out very satisfied with his purchase and anxious to give them to his wife and Leonie was thrilled because the profit on a gift so expensive was more than she would have made on the sale of dozens of small items.

She went to rearrange her display to hide the gap made by the sale of the first of the selection.

When the shop emptied eventually and it seemed there would be no more customers that day Justin and Leonie were satisfied with themselves, the day turning out far happier than either of them had expected.

" It's my turn to treat you Justin, out of the huge profit I've just made on those goblets," she said.

" I'll let you treat me when you've sold the other expensive items for then you'll really see some profit. Your money is tied up in them, you know."

" Don't be mean," she said. " Let me treat you. It's too late tonight, so how about coming back with me to the bungalow and having supper with my mother and aunt. Not very exciting for you, but I would like you to come, and I know they'd like you to."

She was pleased when he accepted her invitation and as they went back to her home she told herself she had never expected to be so happy after having started the day feeling depressed.

It was a change for her mother and aunt to have company. They looked forward to Leonie getting home, and to have a friend of Leonie's as well was quite an event for them and both went to a great deal of trouble to prepare a nice meal for them.

He had brought a bottle of wine in with him and made a great fuss of them, much to their delight. Later, they left him and Leonie alone in the best room to listen to tapes. Leonie had a very good selection and many of them had been brought for her by Justin.

BE—C

He pulled her on to the settee beside him and held her hand. " Let's hold hands 'til love comes," he smiled.

They sat contentedly listening to the music and Justin closed his eyes. Looking at him Leonie knew it wasn't fair of her to sit with him like this unless she intended to satisfy his desire for her. But he seemed quite contented sitting back letting the music soothe him. " Sit back and relax," he said, without opening his eyes, and so she did.

But while she was sitting quietly with Justin she was not thinking of him at all. She was thinking of Mark. If she heard that Mark had married Josy, or his secretary, or anyone at all, she felt the spell of being in love with him would be broken. Then, and then only, would she feel free to fall in love with someone else.

She too, closed her eyes, and she remembered that questioning look in Mark's eyes just before she left as if there was something he wanted to ask her. If only they could have had a good talk together without his trying to hurt her. If only she knew for sure that he was in love with someone else.

How dreadful it would be if she decided to marry Justin, could convince him that she loved him enough to marry him and then discovered that Mark had never stopped loving her, just as she had never stopped loving him.

" You're sitting here with me but you're not with me at all," said Justin at last, opening his eyes.

" How can you say that?" she protested.

" Because I know it's true," he said. " I can sense it. You are quite rigid, look. Not at all relaxed."

" I don't know why you bother with me at all," she said.

" You know quite well why I do," he said. " I shan't be happy until I know you are, either with me or with Mark."

He rose to his feet. " I'm going now, princess. I guess you didn't get a good night's sleep last night, and neither did I, so we'll get an early night."

She went to his car with him and he didn't even offer her

one of his brotherly type kisses. He just said, " Good night, Leonie, see you tomorrow."

" Good night, Justin," she said, and as he went she knew she would sleep much better tonight knowing they were friends again.

FIVE

Leonie had written to Paula to thank her for that lovely week-end when she had stayed with her. She had not expected a reply to her letter immediately for she knew Paula had her hands full looking after her baby and entertaining their many friends.

She often thought of life back in her home town. The sort of life she was living here in Cornwall somehow seemed unreal to her in comparison. She felt as she had always done on a holiday that it was all very nice for a short time, but she had always been glad to return to her normal way of living. Spending all her time in a shop, giving herself to the customers in a sense, wasn't really the kind of life she wanted permanently. She envied Paula who was living a life of domesticity with her little daughter and her husband, though he did work so many hours.

Leonie was making more money than she had ever dreamt she would, but it wasn't giving her any great satisfaction. She couldn't take life leisurely. There was no free time in the summer and in the winter there was little to do in these holiday resorts.

Eventually Paula did get round to answering her letter. She started with apologies for the delay in writing and went on to say that the christening photographs had come out beautifully. ' Mark has to make a trip down south shortly,' she continued, 'and as he has some days holiday still due to him he will call and see you, bringing them for you to see. At the moment someone has borrowed them, but shall get them back so that you can see them too. You looked very nice in that lovely dress you wore and came out very well standing against the church as a background. You have such a tender expression on your face as you look down at my little daughter. Everyone says you are obviously fond of children and it's time you were married and having babies of your own'.

Leonie couldn't concentrate on the rest of the letter which went rambling on for pages more. All she could think about was the part that said, ' Mark will bring the photographs for you to see'. She couldn't imagine from his attitude when he saw her, that he would put himself out that much for her benefit.

She passed over the letter for her mother and her aunt to read and tried to look unaffected when they commented on the fact that Mark would be calling to see her on his travels down their way. But she knew she would be looking for him every day now that she knew he was coming and took extra care with her appearance. It would be awful if he caught her in her shabby jeans and jumpers which she had started to wear now that the weather was cooler. The season was nearly over now, and at times the sea front looked very cold and uninviting. There were still the brave ones who went out surfing and swimming in the unruly waves, but Leonie was not one to spend much time in the sea even when it was really hot. She had never quite got over her childish fear of the sea.

She told Justin that Mark was going to call and see her one of the days with some photographs and he gave her a curious look. " Do you think bringing the photographs might be just an excuse to come and see you? Perhaps he's waiting for you to ask him for your ring back," he said, in a flat voice.

" That's hardly likely," she said.

" I can't see why not," he said. " After all, you are hoping he will offer it back."

Justin was quieter these days. If he noticed that Leonie

was taking extra special care with her appearance and seemed very much on edge he made no comment. Whenever a man came into the shop she looked up full of apprehension.

She was afraid to go out at night, thinking he might call at the bungalow rather than the shop. They didn't keep the shop open so late now that trade wasn't so brisk. She still valued her friendship with Justin above all others and invited him to come to the bungalow often and he accepted her invitations. He was becoming almost like one of the family, and Leonie knew that her mother was fondly hoping that one day soon they would announce their intention of getting married. But Justin didn't mention the subject any more. He seemed happy enough to let things go on as they were. He didn't want to stop seeing Leonie though he knew she had nothing more to offer than friendship.

Leonie felt flattered that he chose to spend his time with her for the girls came flocking to watch Justin at work and it was obvious that many of them would have given anything to gain his attention. Cornwall attracted many artists and writers and it was inevitable that they should come across some of these people. They knew a particularly eccentric female writer and were surprised to learn that her books, which were very outrageous even for these modern times, were best sellers. She lived in a beautiful house high on the cliff tops.

And then Fran was another writer, but so far, not very successful. She came into the shop a great deal, making a friend of Leonie, who knew very well that the real attraction was Justin. She couldn't keep her eyes off him, though she came to talk to Leonie.

Fran told Leonie that she and a friend had found a very old cottage to rent and being told that writers should shut themselves away from other people and become dedicated to their work they had done just that.

" And has it paid off?" asked Leonie.

" Not yet," said Fran, sadly. " We have had one or two

70

successes and perhaps it would have been better if we hadn't had them for we would have packed up and gone back home if it hadn't been for them."

"But small successes lead to better ones," said Leonie, encouragingly.

"That's what we believed when we first came down here. My friend, Angela, was lucky enough to have a novel published and thought she was on the way to fame and fortune, but she hasn't had another accepted since. It was on the strength of that novel and my few successes as a short story writer that we decided to come down here and make our living from writing."

"Are you managing to get enough to eat?" asked Justin, listening in to their conversation.

Fran laughed. "Well, let's say we're not starving. If someone takes us out for a meal it's just heavenly."

"Right," said Justin. "We'll give you and your friend a heavenly evening, eh, Leonie? We'll take you out for a jolly good meal this evening."

Leonie laughed. It would be a pleasure to give someone a treat, and they made arrangements to meet at seven-thirty knowing they would close the shop early.

Fran and her friend Angela arrived in the most way-out clothes imaginable. Angela was wearing a long, drab-looking dress, and Leonie was sure her grandmother wouldn't wear anything like it. Her fair hair was long and straight and she wore huge ear-rings. But she was hilarious. She had them in fits of laughing and Justin said the entertainment they provided more than made up for the cost of the meal. What those two girls put away was amazing. Leonie couldn't finish all of hers so they finished it off between them.

"Perhaps they are eating enough to last them for a few days," Leonie said to Justin, when they were out of hearing range.

But they weren't scroungers. When Justin offered to take them out again a few evenings later Fran said they couldn't possibly accept another free meal so soon. "We'll take you and Leonie out when our ship comes in," she said.

"Well here, take this bag of stale buns off our hands," said Justin, handing her a bag. Leonie smiled at him for she knew he had just been out and bought the contents of that bag and they weren't stale at all.

"Have you thought of getting yourself a job?" asked Leonie one day, when Fran was bemoaning the fact that she had received nothing but rejection slips for weeks from the publishers.

"Well, no," said Fran. "The whole idea was to get down here away from jobs and all that so that we could concentrate on writing. If I wanted a job I might as well go back to my home town where there are plenty of good opportunities for skilled shorthand typists, which I am, you know. I must have been mad to give up my job, I was wealthy back home."

"But you found money wasn't everything, Fran," said Justin.

"Yes I did, but I also discovered that you can't live without it. Being short of money all the time can make life pretty miserable. I suppose eventually we shall have to admit defeat and give in, but we are hanging on for grim death at the moment."

"I know you want to concentrate on your writing but couldn't you take a part-time job? One that didn't take up too much of your time?"

"Well, what could I find in these parts? Now that most of the tourists have gone those with regular employment in the summer are finding themselves with nothing to do at the moment."

"How would you like to help me for a few hours a week?" asked Leonie. "I couldn't give you more than a few hours work at the moment because I'm not doing the trade, but while everything is slack you could be getting to know the stock and the prices so that you could help me next year. My mum and auntie help me out a lot, but there are times

72

when I need even more than their help, especially in the evenings when the shop seems to get more crowded."

Fran's eyes lit up and strayed in Justin's direction. Leonie knew that she would take the opportunity if only to be near Justin more often.

" I'd contribute towards your salary," said Justin, " because I like coffee and you could make more cups for me."

" Great!" cried Fran. " Oh, when can I start? Angela will be delighted if I can earn us a bit of bread. She is in the middle of a new novel, it's very good and I feel sure she'll get this one accepted, so she must stick at it."

" You can start immediately," said Leonie. " I feel like redecorating the shop and you can give me a hand."

" I'll give you a hand as well," said Justin. " You never said you wanted the shop doing up."

" The outside wants doing, the sun has taken the brightness out of the colour and my name isn't at all clear, either. But I shall have to get someone to do that for me."

" Why? I'll do it for you," said Justin.

" Oh, no, I wouldn't dream," she protested. How could she expect a man of independent means like Justin to do the paintwork on her shop? But he insisted and before long he and Fran and Leonie were all working hard giving the shop a new look.

Leonie watched the friendship developing between Fran and Justin. Fran no longer held him in such awe as she had done in the beginning and they laughed and teased each other a lot. Sometimes she wondered if Justin was about to transfer his affections from her to Fran, but when they were alone he would often put his arm around her and give her that special look that told her he loved her. He continued to call her his princess no matter who was around, and Leonie felt he belonged to her. It was rather selfish of her, she admitted, considering that she was not in love with him.

While they were so busy working in the shop Leonie put the thought of Mark's visit out of her mind. It had been several weeks since Paula had written to say he would be coming along with the photographs anyway, and she told herself that it had probably been Paul's idea that he should look her up and not his own. Mark evidently wasn't willing to put himself out to come and see her.

She had no reason to regret asking Fran to come and work part-time for them in the short time she was working in the shop she made her presence felt. She was ready to clear up the mess after they had been colour-washing, or painting, she tidied away the stock, made coffee whenever it was needed, ran errands. There was nothing she wasn't willing to do, and Leonie didn't kid herself that Fran worked herself to death for her. It was Justin she did it for. He had only to mention that he wanted something doing and she was there to do it for him. He seemed highly amused that she was willing to wait on him hand and foot. " I wonder how long it would last if I decided to make her my wife," he said to Leonie, with a grin.

" Probably for always," said Leonie, generously. " She obviously adores you."

" A slave for life," he mused. " If you don't hurry up and marry me, Leonie, I shall be very tempted to take Fran."

" You could do much worse," she told him. " And she'd be lucky if she got you because you wouldn't take advantage of her good nature."

" Ah, Leonie, I don't like to hear you trying to palm me off on to someone else."

" You told me once that my happiness was all that concerned you, Justin," she reminded him. " And I feel the same about you. I want you to be happy."

" But not with someone else, princess," he said, and he looked so utterly sad at the thought that she nearly told him there and then that she'd become his wife.

He had finished the outside painting of the shop and they went out to admire his handiwork. He had painted out the name Leonie, as it had been before, and had made it look more artistic and now standing out clearly. It had previously been painted in red and white and the sun had faded the red to a very pale pink. It looked smarter in black and white and he could see she was pleased with the result as they stood there looking at it, he with his arm around her waist. Fran came and stood beside them, as she was just arriving for her short spell at the shop and she looked wistfully at Justin when she saw the way he was looking at Leonie. How she wished he would look at her in that special way.

" Well, Fran," he said. " It seems we have finished redecorating the shop. Do you like the finished result?"

" Yes," she said. " It's fine."

" I think it calls for a celebration. Do you think Angela could tear herself away from her novel for a few hours one evening this week for a meal."

" I should think so," said Fran, delightedly. " I don't think she'd take much persuading."

The following day she arrived at the shop with a whoop of joy announcing that she had had a short story accepted at long last. " I thought I was never going to sell another one," she declared, " but I have and they're going to pay me forty pounds for it."

" Is that all?" cried Justin. " I thought you'd come in to a fortune."

" It's not the money I'm thrilled about," she said. " It's the fact that I've had another story accepted. It's so disappointing when you get nothing but Editor's Regrets."

" I know how you feel," he said. " When I sell a picture it's not at all the money that thrills me, though it's useful, but the main thing is that someone appreciates your work sufficiently to buy it from you."

Once more Leonie studied these two together and recognized that they had a lot in common. Both were absolutely dedicated to their creative work and she envied them having talents to do something other people admired.

Fran produced the letter telling her that her story was

acceptable and Justin studied it, handing it back to her with a smile. " Well done, Fran!" he said. " You're a clever girl."

" I feel on top of the world for a bit," she said. " I suppose that having this job with Leonie has taken some of the anxiety out of my life and I haven't been quite so worried. Every day I have been desperate for good news, waiting for the post to see if there was a cheque for me, I suppose it's like waiting for the kettle to boil, they say a watched kettle never boils. While I was desperate I had no success, but now I earn a bit and can be more relaxed I might be more successful."

" You are very lucky to have any success at all at your age, Fran," he told her. " Some people persevere for years without any success at all."

" I know. Angela and I belonged to a writers' circle back home and there were so many people there longing to get something published but they never did."

" Did you ask Angela about coming out for a meal tonight? You must celebrate the sale of your story."

" Yes. She'd love to come. Her novel is nearly finished and it's fantastic. I hope she gets that accepted. I want to try my hand at novels later on."

When it was time for her to leave the shop Justin said, " I'll come and pick you girls up at seven so be ready."

" Yes, we will," cried Fran, happily, and went swinging down the street. She had been bubbling over with happiness today. Here was another one whose work meant more to her than anything else, for even though she loved Justin, and knew it was hopeless, the sale of a story could send her into seventh heaven.

Leonie didn't know whether she envied her or not having the talent to write, for there were times when she was in the depths of despair when her work wasn't selling.

It was a wet and dreary day. Leonie didn't like Cornwall in the winter. She supposed it was the dreariness of being

76

stuck in a shop when there was no trade that made her feel depressed. If she was at home in a comfortable house, cooking, looking after her family, keeping the house nice, she wouldn't have to stand and look at the weather so much. Justin didn't seem to be at all affected by the rain. He was beginning to get interested in doing outside paintings now that the tourists were not coming into the shop for their portraits and it seemed to Leonie that he even welcomed the quiet period. Once or twice he had gone off to do some sketching when the sea was particularly rough. He liked to capture those angry waves and storm-tossed boats at sea. He did some remarkable paintings of the fishermen, bringing out their characters so clearly. There was something most serene about the expressions of the weather-beaten men who often risked their lives out at sea.

Soon after Fran had left the shop Justin struggled into his nylon raincoat and announced that he was going to have a look round and Leonie knew he would most probably be away for hours. She tried to interest herself in a paperback romance to pass the time away, and she found herself drinking innumerable cups of coffee for something to do.

However, her day was brightened when a customer came in for a special gift which was to be presented to the matron of the hospital on her retirement. She said she had noticed the display of lovely cut glass and came to examine it more thoroughly. She took a long time to make up her mind and then settled on a cut-glass vase which was nearly thirty pounds. Leonie had been very doubtful about buying it, but was now delighted to have a purchaser. She placed it in the box with layers of tissue and carefully wrapped it for her satisfied customer, who counted out the money which had been collected by the staff of the hospital for this retirement gift.

" I'm sure she'll be happy with that," she told her customer.

" I do hope so. I think it's beautiful."

Leonie found she was almost as thrilled over this sale as Fran had been over the sale of her story, and as soon as Justin returned looking rosy-faced after being out in the cold wind and rain, she told him excitedly about the sale. " I was sitting here most depressed," she said. " I felt it was waste of time opening the shop during the winter and then I sold that expensive cut-glass vase."

" And your profit on that is worth having," he smiled. " You missed me, that's why you were depressed," he said. " Let me show you what I have been doing."

He unwrapped the waterproof covering from his block and showed her several fishermen at work repairing their nets even though the weather was bitingly cold. " Justin, you're a genius! I'm sure your work is getting better all the time," she told him.

" I have a lot of work to do on these yet," he said. " These are only rough sketches. I want to paint them in oils. See, I've made a note of the colour of their clothes and so on."

Leonie realized that Justin, like Fran and Angela would want to shut himself away and work in solitude on these pictures. " I suppose you'll not be coming to the shop so much now you have these to concentrate on, and the portrait business has fallen off a bit."

" Well," he said, slowly. " I could do with spending some time in my own studio, but if you are going to be depressed sitting here on your own . . ."

" Don't think about me," she said, hastily. " I'd hate to think you were neglecting your work on my account."

She regretted now that she had mentioned she had been depressed for Justin was the type to consider people he thought a lot of too much. He had worked for his father for years because he knew his father needed him, and he'd done work in which he had no interest at all. She didn't want him to neglect his work on her account, though she knew it would be a little dead in the shop without his presence."

" I could do with a coffee," he said, rubbing his hands

together. " I'm frozen. It's a pity my little slave isn't here," he grinned.

" Well you've got another little slave here," she said, with an exaggerated sigh. " I'll go and make you a coffee."

He was deep in the study of his afternoon's work when Leonie went up to the shop again with the coffee. She handed him his cup and he sipped it gratefully, still contemplating his studies of the fishermen.

" Fine men," he said, putting his free arm round Leonie's shoulder. " I love to listen to the stories they have to tell. I've often wondered how they have the nerve to go out on the sea in dangerously rough weather, but they all seem to have stories about some supernatural presence that gives them courage to face danger."

" I've heard that soldiers in battle have had the same feeling. That there is a presence that has been with them in danger, protecting them," said Leonie.

" I believe them," said Justin. " These men are too sincere and too strong in character to be spinning a yarn. I think that because they are aware of protecting powers they are better people than the rest of us. You see this man here." He pointed to an elderly man with deep lines in his face but such a wonderful expression. " He is a member of the life-boat crew. He has escaped death many times, I've been told and has helped to bring in many many ship-wrecked sailors who have been in great danger."

" And you've got all that character in your sketch of him, Justin. There is more beauty in a weather-lined face like that than in the face of a beautiful girl who has never been touched by trouble or sorrow."

" I'm glad you think that," he said. " That's how I feel, and when I am sketching I aim to get that wonderful expression. Perhaps you'll think I'm being fanciful when I tell you that I often feel a guiding hand helping me to get what I want."

" Do you really, Justin?" she asked, her eyes alight. " Why

79

that's marvellous. I suppose that's when you get true genius."

He laughed. " I'm glad you think I'm a genius."

" I'm not an expert judge," she said, " but I do know that your sketches and paintings have an effect on me when the work of others often leaves me cold. Back home there was a display once of paintings and water-colours done automatically, like automatic writing. They were shown in the local art gallery. The artist claimed that the work was not his own. They were done by someone guiding him and they were absolutely beautiful. There was one of Christ and I've never forgotten the expression in the eyes. They seemed to look straight at you with love, compassion, understanding, oh, I can't express how many things. I just stood spellbound and wanted to cry. And when I look at some of your work I can see that you too are able to get the most wonderful expression in the eyes of your subject."

" I would have liked to see that display in your local art gallery," he said.

" He called himself a psychic artist," said Leonie. " There was an article about him in the local paper. There were a lot of people who said it was a load of rubbish. They didn't go to see the paintings in the art gallery, of course. If they had done they would have seen that the pictures were remarkable whether they had been done automatically, or otherwise. Why would a man who could paint like that claim that he hadn't done them himself if it wasn't true? He refused to part with any of them for cash he valued them so much."

" It would be nice to see him at work."

" Yes, fascinating I should think for he claimed that the most wonderful paintings were completed in about half an hour."

" Although I often feel a guiding hand I like to think that I have a skill of my own," said Justin. " It wouldn't be such a thrill to me to know that someone else was responsible for my work. I'm grateful for help, you know, but I want to be the painter, not have a painter working through me no matter how brilliant a painter."

Leonie looked at him thoughtfully. "But I suppose we could do nothing on our own," she said. "Perhaps we are all being helped all the time but are not aware of it."

"Hi, this is getting too deep for me," he said. He looked at his watch. "I think it's time we started to pack up to go home. I'm regretting now that I arranged for that meal tonight, I'd love to go back home and work all through the night on my paintings while the pictures of the men are still clear in my mind."

"We couldn't disappoint Fran and Angela," she said.

"Or you," he smiled. "No I wouldn't dream of doing that, but I wish I could have had tonight free to get cracking, I'm impatient to start."

As Leonie washed out their coffee cups and put everything away neat and tidy in the kitchen she was thinking about Justin. She could understand now his desire to be free. He would be completely happy tonight without any company while he got on with his work which meant such a lot to him.

She supposed that during the last months while he had spent such a lot of time with her he had managed to put his work in the background, but now he was yearning to get back to it again. Whoever Justin married they would have to understand that he needed his freedom, his solitude to create those wonderful pictures. Artists are supposed to be difficult to live with, she remembered, but that was perhaps believed by those who would not leave them in peace to work when the desire for work was strong.

When she went back upstairs Justin was putting in a little touch here and there to his sketches. Without speaking to him she got her coat and handbag then she stood beside him for a moment before going to switch off the lights and his arm came round over her shoulder.

"Shan't be a moment, love," he said.

She saw someone outside stand and look up at the name

over the shop and although she couldn't see too clearly because it was dark outside, she found the blood beginning to pound in her head. There was something very familiar about the stance of that man out there, and when he came to the door and opened it she was in no doubt at all. She steeled herself to remain calm, but Justin could feel her body going rigid beneath his hand on her shoulder.

"What's the matter, princess?" he asked, without looking up from his sketch.

But she didn't hear him. She was looking at the man before her, and her voice came out in a croak.

"Mark! I didn't expect to see you at this time in the day."

She felt Justin's hand tighten on her shoulder as she spoke Mark's name and saw that he noticed for his eyes rested on Justin's hand.

"I went to the bungalow and your mother told me where to find your shop," said Mark.

Justin was looking at Mark intently now. "Justin, this is Mark, Mark Trueman. Mark, this is Justin Lewis."

The two men looked at each other, weighing each other up, before Mark held out his hand, and Justin reached out to shake hands with him.

SIX

Ever since Leonie had had Paula's letter to say that Mark was coming down to bring the photographs she had put herself out to look her best and told herself she would be in complete control of herself when he arrived, but after so long she had given up hope of seeing him and he had caught her unawares, looking anything but her best, and his gaze rested on Justin's hand firmly gripping her shoulder. She began to babble, nervously.

" Paula told me you were coming, but it's been so long ago I thought you weren't after all, especially now that the nice weather has gone, it's hardly the right time for a holiday . . ."

" I intended to come a week or so ago," said Mark, " but the man I had to see at a firm just outside Plymouth has been abroad and I have had to wait until he got back."

" Are you intending to stay in this area?" asked Justin.

" Well, I booked into the Dolphin Hotel, I suppose you know it, a small place, but quite comfortable. I don't know whether I shall stay more than a couple of days, it all depends."

" You could have stayed with us, my aunt would have been pleased to accommodate you. Paula and Ron stayed with us earlier in the year," said Leonie.

" Yes, she told me, but I felt I couldn't impose. Paula is your special friend, after all."

" Oh, Mark," said Leonie, reproachfully. " You know you would have been welcome."

She saw Mark's eyes look down at Justin's pictures on the counter, and she said eagerly, " Would you like to see

Justin's work? I think these sketches are marvellous."

Justin turned the sketches around for him to look at and Mark studied them with care. "These are fine," he said. "Excellent. They look alive. I'm afraid I haven't any artistic talents at all. You have a wonderful gift, it must give you a great deal of satisfaction to be able to catch people like that, so naturally."

"It's an obsession with me, isn't it, Leonie?" said Justin. "I'm never happy unless I'm painting or sketching."

Mark looked at them both, uncertainly. "I suppose you were just off, both of you, seeing you have your outdoor clothes on?"

"We are leaving a little early because we're going out tonight with a couple of friends, just for a meal. Would you like to join us, Mark?" asked Leonie.

"Would you mind?" he said, addressing Justin more than Leonie.

"No, come by all means, the more the merrier," said Justin. "I'll let them know there will be an extra one. We're going to the Galleon, they put on a good meal there."

Leonie looked from one to the other. "Perhaps Mark could come back with me to the bungalow, Justin, and we'll meet at the Galleon, later."

"Right," said Justin, but Leonie was sure he wasn't very pleased about that arrangement at all.

She turned off the lights and locked the shop, and they went their various ways. When she sat in the car with Mark she remembered the days when this had been an every-day occurrence. The car Mark had had then was much shabbier than this luxurious model he was using now.

"I like your car," she said.

"Actually it belongs to my firm but I am allowed to use it as my own which is quite an advantage. I have no repair bills, no running costs at all, and when I've had this a couple of years it will automatically be changed for another."

"That's worth quite a lot on top of your salary," she remarked.

"One of the perks of a director," he smirked. "I like your shop," he went on. "How long have you known that artist fellow?"

"Justin? Oh, almost a year. He came and asked if he could do portraits in my shop. He thought it might bring customers in for me, having the attraction of an artist on the premises."

"And save him the cost of a studio," said Mark, dryly.

"Oh, Justin's not like that," she protested, disliking his tone. "He offered to pay me quite a generous sum for a trial period and it's worked out well for both of us. When he does exceptionally well he always offers me extra for allowing him to use the shop which I wouldn't accept, for we made an agreement which suits me very well. He makes it up by buying me presents or taking me out for an evening, like tonight."

She went on to tell him all the good things about Justin. How well he did with his portraits, how he had worked with his father for years when all the time he had wanted to be an artist, but when his father died he had sold up the business and was living as he had always wanted to. "Actually, he's quite wealthy, I believe. He told me he needn't work for his living."

"And he's in love with you, of course?"

The colour rushed to her face and he said, "I knew that as soon as I saw you together. Has he asked you to marry him, or doesn't he believe in marriage? Artists don't, do they?"

"If you're suggesting that Justin gets favours from me without marriage you're quite wrong," she retorted, angrily. "He isn't that type at all. As a matter of fact he has asked me to marry him."

"Has he? Well there's no need to get all flustered and upset about it."

"I'm not," she said, knowing perfectly well that he had

85

angered her, and she supposed she had gone on and on about Justin.

" When's the wedding to be?" he asked.

" I haven't said there's going to be a wedding," she snapped.

" Are you afraid of marriage?" he asked. " You dropped me, then Eliot, and now you're keeping this poor chap on tenterhooks."

" There's plenty of time," she said. " I'm not an old spinster yet. I'm only twenty-three."

" So you are. It seems so long since you broke off our engagement that I was thinking you were much older."

They had arrived at the bungalow now and Leonie got out of the car quickly and slammed the door behind her as she went to go indoors. He caught her up and took her hand. " Sorry, Leonie," he said. " You look very young and beautiful. Let's be friends while I'm here, shall we?"

She looked at him, her eyes beginning to fill with tears. " Yes," she muttered, but she wanted much more than friendship from Mark and seeing him again was filling her with all the old longings for him.

" I haven't prepared very much for you tonight," said Mrs. Drew, anxiously when she saw Leonie had returned with Mark. " You told us not to bother as you were going out."

" That's right, Mum. Don't worry. We are going out."

" Mark as well?"

" Yes, he's coming with us."

" You're quite welcome to anything, Mark," said Mrs. Drew. " It's just that I wasn't prepared."

" That's all right," he said. " Thanks."

Her mother followed her as she went into her bedroom and she whispered, " Has he met Justin, then?"

" Yes," said Leonie. " They met in the shop."

" I wondered whether I'd done the right thing in sending him to the shop."

" Why of course you did," said Leonie.

" Mark's changed," said her mother. " The last time I saw him he seemed like a boy, but now he's a man."

" Well, he is older," smiled Leonie. " It has been two years since you saw him."

Her mother looked at her anxiously. " Justin isn't going to be pleased to have Mark tagging along with you."

" He hasn't anything to worry about," said Leonie. " Mark is this way on business and called on his way back home, that's all."

Her mother gave a sigh. " Are you disappointed?" asked Leonie. " Do you prefer Mark to Justin?"

" I don't know," she said, a little bewildered. " I like them both. I wouldn't want to hurt either of them."

" Neither would I," said Leonie. " But Mark is not interested in me any more, Mum, so he'll be all right. He's been asking me when I am to marry Justin."

When she had put her things away she returned to the sitting-room where Mark was sitting comfortably by the cosy fire with a cup of tea and some interesting-looking sandwiches on a plate.

" Here's yours, Leonie," said her aunt. " I put them on this little table here. We thought that would be suitable for a little snack to keep you going until you arrive for your meal out."

" Yes, that's lovely, thanks," said Leonie. She turned to Mark. " What about these photographs you've brought for me to see?"

" Oh, yes, I forgot," he said, fumbling in his inside pocket for his wallet. He produced them and she began to study them, and show them around to her mother and her aunt. " That was a lovely day," said Leonie. " See how the sun was shining, Mum. Isn't that a good one of the baby?"

" Good of you, too," said Mark, meeting her eyes. She lowered hers quickly, afraid he might see the love in her eyes which she had for him.

87

When she handed the photographs back he said, " No, keep them. They're for you."

" So many," she said. " I must pay for them. It costs the earth to have films developed these days."

" Don't be ridiculous," he said. " As if we would charge you for them."

" Paula and the baby okay?" she asked.

" Yes, they're fine, thanks," he said. " The baby is coming on great, she's nothing like she appears on the snaps now, you know. Paula wishes you lived nearer. She misses you."

" I miss her too," said Leonie, with a sigh.

" But you wouldn't want to leave Cornwall now, would you? There are so many things to keep you here. Your shop, Justin, and these other friends you have made. What are the girls' names?"

" Fran and Angela. They're writers," said Leonie. " Living in poverty almost, but so anxious to be successful writers. Fran had a story accepted this week and she's been on top of the world, but her successes are few and far between."

" You do meet interesting people," he commented.

She jumped up quickly after glancing at her watch. " Goodness, I must get ready," she said, and dashed off to change.

Mark had no need to change he already looked very smart in a tan-coloured suit with a cream shirt and tan-coloured tie. And she had to admit that she liked his clean shaven, fresh-coloured face more than Justin's dark complexion and often too bushy beard. Mark was entirely different from Justin. Like herself, he admired the artists, but had no talent at all in that direction.

She looked through her wardrobe and decided to really go to town tonight. She had a lovely delicate blue evening gown which she had only worn once when she was going out with Mark. She decided to wear that and see if he would remember it. The necklace which matched it was one that he had given her—would he recognize that as well?

She studied the finished result when she was ready and knew she was rather overdressed for the Galleon, but she hadn't been able to resist the temptation to make herself look her best for Mark's benefit.

"Goodness knows what I shall look like in contrast to Fran and Angela's way-out clothes," she told herself, but with a final look at herself and a pat to her fair hair, she went out to let Mark see she was ready.

He was still in the easy chair glancing through the paper and he looked up casually when she came into the room, but his eyes rested on her for quite a time, and time seemed to stand still, until he said, "Oh, you're ready," and jumped up from the chair, leaving the paper behind him.

She had a short fur coat, very light and soft which she felt she could wear over her dress tonight for the temperature was definitely low. And then as they went out to Mark's car she wished she hadn't dressed up so elaborately. Justin would know she had done it for Mark's benefit, and the young girls would be amazed to see her looking so elegantly dressed just for an ordinary meal out.

"You look very nice," said Mark, as he started the car. "Your boy-friend will be wishing he had you all to himself instead of having others included in the party."

She looked at him in annoyance. She hadn't dressed up for Justin, it was for Mark's benefit, and he was merely being sarcastic.

They travelled in silence after she had given him directions for reaching the Galleon. "Cheer up," he said, when they were nearly there. "I shall soon be on my way back home so you won't have to put up with my presence for long. It was good of you to ask me to come along tonight, seeing that you aren't keen on my company."

"Stop it, Mark," she said. "I didn't ask you out of politeness. I wanted you to come and you asked me to agree to be friends, remember?"

"Sorry, but you are so quiet I thought you resented my

coming along with you."

"We're nearly there," she said. "You won't make any nasty comments in front of my friends, will you?"

"Have I ever done that?" he asked.

"Well, not when friends have been around, but you were pretty nasty when I came to stay with Paula. If you remember you completely ignored me the first evening I was there."

"I shouldn't have thought that would have bothered you."

"It wasn't very nice," she said. "At least you could pretend to like me when there are other people present."

"Very well, princess," he said, mockingly.

"Don't you dare call me that in front of Justin making fun of him," she cried, angrily. "At least he treats me with respect."

"Yes, your royal highness. I'll do my best to behave."

She began to see it had been a mistake to ask Mark to come along, and she regretted so much that she had gone to the trouble to make herself look beautiful for his benefit. He was parking the car now and she looked up at him anxiously as she got out of the car and waited for him to lock it. He looked down at her and suddenly put his arm round her and drew her close. "Don't worry, Leonie. Enjoy yourself. I won't do anything to spoil things for you and Justin."

She looked at him seriously and he said, impatiently, "For goodness sake don't look as if you're going to be thrown to the lions. You don't truthfully imagine I'm going to do anything to come between you and him, do you?"

She looked down and he put his finger under her chin to lift her face to his again. "You look very lovely, tonight. That's how I've remembered you in my dreams." He put his lips to hers and gave her a light kiss. "Come on, smile now," he said, and took her arm as they walked towards the Galleon.

Justin and the girls were already waiting at the bar having a drink and when Mark and Leonie arrived Justin came

90

forward immediately and took charge of her possessively. She saw from his expression that he had noticed she had dressed herself up more than usual and his smile showed he appreciated her appearance.

Fran and Angela were dressed in their usual striking out-fits. Angela this time, instead of wearing a drab, dreary-looking dress, wore a floral dress in brilliant colours and it seemed to have no shape in it at all. Fran wore a long full skirt with a deep frill on the hem and a red off the shoulder blouse. If Mark thought their clothes were unusual to say the least, he didn't show it. He was introduced to the girls and gave them charming smiles which won them over immediately. Leonie could see that they thought he was wonderful, and so did she.

" Leonie tells me that you two girls write for a living," he said.

" A very poor living at the moment," laughed Fran. " We're managing mainly on a salary Leonie pays me for working part-time in her shop."

" Don't forget the forty pounds you received this week for a short story, Fran," said Justin.

" It does give one a boost," said Fran. " We're hoping that Angela's novel sells. I think it's very good so far."

" What are you having to drink, Mark?" asked Justin.

" Let's see," said Mark, accompanying him to the bar, and while they were getting drinks all round Fran and Angela began to tell Leonie how good-looking Mark was. " He's very fond of you," said Angela. " You're lucky having two boy-friends. I haven't got one."

" Well, you can't spend all your time writing masterpieces and be out looking for a boy-friend," laughed Leonie.

" I wouldn't get anyone like Justin or Mark to look at me, anyway," she said. " I'm love-starved you know. That's why I write about love. They say that women who write love stories are usually love-starved."

Leonie laughed. " I've never heard that before. What

91

about men who write stories about criminals? What's wrong with them do they reckon?"

" Probably they would like to be criminals themselves and haven't the nerve," said Angela.

The men returned and then the waiter came to tell them their table was ready and off they went into the dining-room.

Conversation was never dull with Angela. She soon had them all laughing with the stories she told, mostly against herself. She never minded telling anyone about the bricks she dropped in company, or the times when she had made a fool of herself. She gave the impression that she was a real zany person, but in reality she was quite a clever girl and Leonie hoped she would have some success soon with her writing.

When the subject of writing came up she told them she had several books out for consideration with different publishers. " But it takes some of them months to make up their mind. Just when I think they must be going to make me an offer for it or they would have returned it, it comes back with a plop through the letter box. One novel was lost for ages. I wrote repeatedly for its return if they were not interested in it, and then eventually it came back all dog-eared and tattered and they told me they were very sorry but it had been discovered under the typist's cushion. She had used it to make her seat higher."

" I don't believe you," laughed Mark.

" It's true, isn't it, Fran?" she said, solemnly. " I never fancied that manuscript again after that unknown typist had had her bottom on it for weeks."

" I've told her to iron it out and send it off on its travels again. I often iron my manuscripts out smoothly when they are returned looking the worse for wear, and they go out again looking like new. The story I have just had accepted had been to several magazines before it finally got accepted."

They wined and dined well and finished with coffee laced

with brandy. And then they were content to sit and talk. " It's a pity they don't have dancing here," said Justin. " I wonder if there's anywhere we could get in for a dance at this time of night."

" I doubt it," said Fran. " There's not much doing around here once the season has finished."

" Let's go back to our place and dance to some records," said Angela.

The fellows agreed, and Leonie said she would like to see this cottage of theirs so they got up to go. Mark and Justin went to get a bottle of wine to take with them. " If Justin goes first with Fran and I to show the way," said Angela, " Mark can follow and bring you Leonie."

Leonie agreed that that was a good idea but she saw that Justin didn't think so at all, but he needed the girls to show him where they lived, and they couldn't very well leave Mark to follow on his own.

From Fran's description of the old cottage Leonie expected it to be a tumble-down old place and she warned Mark that it might be so, but they had a pleasant surprise when they came upon it. It was very old, admittedly, but it had a charm of its own, though they couldn't get a good impression of it late at night. Inside it was beautifully cosy. The girls had made it into a really comfortable home and there were indoor flowering plants in the tiny hall and in the sitting-room. They switched on their electric fire which had a log-fire effect and then Angela and Fran sorted out some records. Their taste in music was way-out, the same as their clothes, but it was a nice atmosphere sitting there in the dim light of a standard lamp, and they all sat round contentedly.

Mark was so comfortable he nearly dropped off to sleep and Leonie learned that he had travelled all the way down to Plymouth that day, had had an interview with the man he wanted to see, and then travelled on here so no wonder he was tired.

Fran and Angela started to do some weird dancing to the

music and seeing that Mark was almost asleep they pulled Justin to his feet and got him to join in their strange dances too. " I wouldn't do it if I hadn't had more than I should to drink," he said, acting the fool with them.

" Mark, you are tired," said Leonie, in concern. " I think you ought to go to your hotel and get some sleep."

He roused himself and looked around as if it surprised him to find himself in the cottage. " Yes, I think I'll be making tracks. You don't mind if I get off, do you? I've had a very good evening thanks to you all, but I shall disgrace myself and fall fast asleep if I don't go."

Leonie rose to go with him thinking he would drop her off at the bungalow, but he pushed her back on her seat. " No need for you to leave the party," he said. " Justin will see you home, I'm sure."

" Of course, Mark," said Justin. " I wouldn't expect you to take her, anyway."

Leonie felt most annoyed. Mark spoke as if she was Justin's property and Justin was making it look that way as well.

They watched Mark drive away after he had wished them all good night. " Shall we be seeing you again?" asked Fran.

" I don't know," he said. " I might be getting back home tomorrow. I've gained the information I required when I came down this way."

Leonie looked at him in dismay and he looked at her for a moment, and then he was on his way. He'd never even wished her good-bye. She didn't know how she would find the strength to go back into the cottage and not break down in tears.

Justin must have understood how she felt for he said, " I think we'll call it a day too, Leonie, it's getting late."

Fran fetched Leonie's lovely fur coat and held it against her cheek. " This is beautiful," she said, " It must have cost a fortune."

" It was a twenty-first birthday present," said Leonie.

" From my mother."

Fran held it up for her to put on, and after thanking them for a lovely evening she and Justin left them too.

" All this was for his benefit, wasn't it?" said Justin, touching her dress as they drove away.

" I've had the dress for a long time," she said. " I don't see why I shouldn't have worn it tonight."

" Has he seen you in it before?"

" Yes. But it made no difference. Mark didn't come down here specially to see me. He said he had discovered what he intended, from his business colleague, I gathered, and he'll be on his way back tomorrow. I don't even know whether he intends to see me again before he goes."

" Do you still want him when he can treat you so casually?" he asked, angrily.

" How did you expect him to behave?" she asked. " You made it look perfectly obvious that I was your girl."

" Are you?"

" You know very well I'm not, Justin. You know how I have felt about Mark all the time. I haven't tried to lead you on in any way. You know I'm not in love with you, but you made Mark think there was something special between us."

" I could curse his coming back and disturbing you. We were so happy this afternoon talking about painting and so forth. I felt you were beginning to be serious about me and then he had to walk in spoiling everything."

" How can he have spoilt anything when he isn't even interested in me?"

" He's made you restless again, and it's not giving you a chance to forget him seeing him like this."

" I'd be a fool to go on yearning for him if he goes tomorrow without even saying good-bye to me," she said, sadly.

" I hope you don't see him again."

" Justin if you truly loved me you would want what is best for me, and if I want Mark you should accept that. As it happens I have no chance with him. It seems he has a wife already in mind and it's not me. I wouldn't want him knowing he loved someone else. But you didn't help today. Mark is convinced there is something between us two, and if he had wanted me you would have spoilt my chances."

"You can't blame me for trying to win you for myself."

"Would it please you to know you had gained me if you knew I wanted someone else and you'd prevented me having him?"

He was silent and she knew he was thinking about that. When they reached the bungalow he stopped and turned towards her. "Do you think Mark actually came down here to see you and ask you to go back to him?"

"No," she said. "I'm sure he didn't. He wasn't all that nice to me when we were on our own. We agreed to behave as if we were friends this evening for the sake of the rest of you."

"And yet you made yourself look beautiful for him. He must be mad not to see how much he means to you."

They sat in silence and suddenly he put his arm around her and pulled her close to him. "Leonie," he said, brokenly, "I love you so much. I hate you to be unhappy. I'd never hurt you. He does, and yet you want him."

She rested her head against Justin's chest. "How can I understand why I feel as I do?" she said. "It's just something inside me that won't let me fall in love with you. Perhaps I'm immune to love now. It's like people who get vaccinated, isn't it? Once they've been injected they can't get the disease again. I must be like that. I can't love again."

He hugged her close and started to laugh. "I've never heard of love being classed as a disease before," he said.

She laughed with him and for a time she let him hold her close to him, then at last she drew away. "I must go, Justin, it's very late."

Reluctantly he released her. "I could hold you like this forever."

"Perhaps you should stop seeing me," she suggested. "You tell me I should forget Mark and seeing him is bad for me. You should stop seeing me and then you'd forget me."

"I'll never forget you," he said. "Even if I never win your love I'll never forget you."

She thought for a moment he was going to call her princess and she began to giggle thinking of Mark referring to her as her royal highness. Mark used to have a wonderful sense of humour, but since she'd broken her engagement to him, his humour had turned to sarcasm and cynicism.

"Why are you laughing?" asked Justin, offended.

"It was nothing," she said. "I just thought of something funny."

"When I was being so much in earnest," he complained.

"I know, I shouldn't have laughed. That's another thing I don't understand. Why, in the middle of a serious happening should one suddenly think about something funny. I used to do that at school and the teacher used to be furious when I couldn't stop laughing in the middle of something very serious."

He hugged her. "I'd rather leave you in fits of laughing than in tears," he said. "I'll try to think of something funny on the way home to make me laugh."

They were both laughing when he drove away, but it was a sad Leonie who hung her lovely evening dress in the wardrobe and wondered if she would ever wear it again. She had had such hopes that it would bring back happy memories for Mark and make him want her again.

She lay in bed for a long time thinking about him. Could he set off home tomorrow without giving her another thought?

He had looked so tired tonight. It would be better for him to have a rest tomorrow instead of taking that long journey back home so soon. She couldn't sleep, although she was tired. If only Mark had held her cradled in his arms as

Justin had just done. She would just about die with happiness if Mark decided he loved her after all. When he had put their engagement ring on her finger Leonie had given herself to Mark as if they were married, and she couldn't believe they no longer belonged to each other.

When morning came she felt wretched. She could hardly bring herself to get up and start another day. Her mother brought her a cup of tea and sat by the bed for a chat. " Did you have a nice evening last night?" she asked. " Auntie and I thought you had never looked lovelier than you did when you went out, and Mark looked at you as if he thought you were wonderful too."

" I'm sure he didn't," said Leonie. " You imagined that. He wasn't even pleasant to me when we went out."

She turned her mother's thoughts away from Justin and Mark by talking about Fran and Angela and their lovely little cottage. " Fran told me it was a terribly old cottage, but I thought it was really lovely."

" Some of the old buildings round here will outlast the houses they are putting up in the Midlands," said her mother. " They're built of granite and meant to last."

Her mother left her in order to go and start the breakfast. Leonie left her tea untouched. She lay back on her pillow wishing she needn't get up and start another day. Her mother called to tell her it was late, but she didn't care. Justin had a key to the shop if he should arrive before her so no one would be put out very much if she arrived late.

SEVEN

Leonie continued to lie in bed thinking about her future. She suddenly knew that she didn't want her shop any more. It was better to sell it and go away. It wasn't fair to Justin to see him every day when she had no intention of marrying him. Mark was probably on his way home and she felt most hurt about that. He hadn't even said good night to her last night, let alone good-bye.

She felt so down-hearted she couldn't bring herself to get up, have her breakfast and go to the shop. What could she do with her life? The sale of her shop would bring her some capital to tide her over for a time, and she had some savings for she had made good profits over the year and hadn't had time to spend a great deal, so she had plenty of time to make up her mind what she wanted to do.

If only she could get away on her own to sort things out. Her mother and her aunt had always been sympathetic and she appreciated their concern over her unhappiness, but she didn't want any more sympathy. Perhaps she could work her way round the world. She had a cousin in Australia who had twice been round the world, snatching work in the big cities until she had sufficient to take her on the next step of the way. Leonie had always envied her cousin having the nerve to do that all on her own, but now she wondered if she could do it herself. It would be a challenge and perhaps get all the unhappiness out of her system. She had grieved long enough over Mark.

Mrs. Drew came into her room looking at her anxiously. " Are you all right, love? Your breakfast has been ready ages, and it's well after nine."

"I'm coming," said Leonie, and slipped out of bed to take a shower. Without being at all interested in what she wore she chose a polo-neck green jumper, and her jeans.

Her aunt and her mother fussed around thinking that maybe she was ill or something. It was not like her to hang around the house like this when she should be at the shop. Leonie had several cups of coffee but could only manage to eat a small piece of toast leaving her mother and her sister to eat the breakfast they had cooked for her ' to save wasting it ' they said. " But I'm already putting on too much weight," said Mrs. Drew.

" I want to talk to you both," said Leonie. " Would you be very upset if I decided to sell my shop and leave Cornwall?"

They both looked at her in amazement. " You can't mean that?" said her mother. " It's a marvellous little business for you."

" It's a good business for anyone," said Leonie, " but I'm tired of it. I want to travel a bit before I make up my mind what I'd rather do. I'm beginning to wish I'd gone to university now and studied for a career."

" It's not too late is it?" asked her aunt. " You aren't very old, and you got your ' A ' levels didn't you?"

" No, I'm afraid I only got ' O ' levels, Auntie. Paula and I decided we didn't want to go to university so there was no point in studying for ' A ' levels."

" You have to live your own life," said her mother. " We should miss you if you went away. And we should miss the shop. It has given us quite an interest helping out when you've been busy, but I'm afraid it might be too much for us to run on our own."

" Couldn't we get someone to help us?" asked Aunt Louise. " Leonie has Fran helping her out. Perhaps Angela would help part-time as well, and with someone to help cook for us and clean the bungalow we could run the shop ourselves."

Leonie looked at them thoughtfully. They weren't old by any means. There were many people of their age running small businesses.

" If you decided to buy the shop from me I would naturally let you have it for less than I would take from a stranger," said Leonie, " but you must take your time in thinking about it. There are lots of things to take into consideration. There's the book-keeping for one thing, and the V.A.T. to be considered."

" I used to be a book-keeper years ago," smiled Aunt Louise. " I was quite good at it. I would soon pick it up again, and I like keeping accounts. I should be thrilled to have the shop with your mother if you've really made up your mind to sell it."

" But we should miss you, Leonie," said her mother, " I know we don't see a great deal of you, but we do see you every day, and know you are near. Where are you thinking of going?"

" Round the world," said Leonie, dryly.

" Round the world!" cried her mother. " Who with?"

" By myself. Like Caroline has done. She's not at all interested in getting married. She loves travelling. She told us so. And as soon as she's earned sufficient she sets off round the world."

" But they earn more money to begin with in Australia," said her mother.

" Caroline has been broke many times," said Leonie. " She takes a job doing anything in order to carry on. She worked in a fish and chip shop once, and another time as a waitress, and has even cleaned offices. She doesn't mind what she does because she knows it's only for a short time, just long enough for her to save the fare to move on to the next city or perhaps another country. You could see she was finding life grand."

" I'm sure her mother would be happier if she were to

settle down," said Mrs. Drew.

"I daresay she would," said Leonie, "but it's Caroline's life to do as she chooses. If she wanted to settle down she has had plenty of opportunities. She's a good-looking girl, and when I went out with her once or twice the last time she was over she got on quite well with the boys we met."

Her mother sighed. "Girls are not like they were in my day."

"There weren't the opportunities in your day, Mum, for girls to go round the world. Few men had the chance unless they were in the services, and you can't blame people for seeing all they can of this planet before they have to leave it."

"Oh, Leonie, if you try to do what Caroline has done I'll be worried to death, you're not like her. You wouldn't have the same confidence."

"I don't suppose Caroline had so much confidence when she first started on her travels," said Aunt Louise. "She must have gained it as she went along."

"It's all right for you, Louise," said Mrs. Drew. "Leonie's not your daughter. Leonie's all I've got."

"You've got me," said Louise, "and we've got years ahead of us yet to enjoy ourselves. If Leonie does sell the shop to us we can make a lot of money and then we'll go round the world. Not working our way, we'll travel in style."

Leonie had to laugh at her aunt's light-heartedness. She knew she was only trying to make her mother feel less sad at the thought of her daughter going away, but she was making a good job of it.

"Won't Justin wonder where you are this morning?" asked her mother. "Or did you tell him you wouldn't be going to the shop today? You haven't quarrelled, have you?"

"No, Mum. It's because of Justin I thought of giving up the shop and going away. He wants me to marry him, and if I see him every day and have to keep telling him I don't want to it's not very nice, and it's not fair to keep seeing him either."

" Poor Justin. But still, love, you shouldn't have to sell your shop because you don't want to see him. You should tell him it's not convenient for him to share your shop premises any more."

" Hark, who's talking," said Leonie. " Could you tell Justin that?"

" No, I suppose not. I can see how awkward it is for you."

" I'd better go to the shop now and tell him I've decided to sell up and move on. That's going to be difficult enough."

" I thought you were getting to like him a lot," said her aunt.

" She was," said her mother. " It's Mark coming back that's made her unsettled."

Leonie didn't answer that. She decided to have a sharp walk to warm herself up, for it wasn't so warm in the shop these days, though the strongly built Cornish buildings remained warmer in winter and cooler in summer than the ordinary brick buildings in other parts of the country.

She had never been so late getting to the shop and expected to see Justin there when she arrived for it was almost midday, but the shop was closed and Fran was waiting outside looking bored and cold.

" Oh, Fran, have you been waiting long?" asked Leonie, in concern. " I expected Justin to be here."

" I haven't seen him," said Fran, rubbing her hands together. " It's rather bleak isn't it being so near to the sea?"

" Yes, I'm so sorry. I would have come sooner if I'd known Justin wasn't coming. There's not a lot of trade this time of the year so I wasn't too bothered about getting here early. I very nearly took the whole day off."

" I thought perhaps you had decided to got out with Mark," said Fran.

103

" No," said Leonie, sadly. " He's on his way home today. I was engaged to Mark once, you know. I broke off the engagement through a stupid quarrel and have regretted it ever since."

Leonie bent down to switch on the electric fire so that they could warm their hands.

" But you are still friends?" said Fran.

" Not very good friends," said Leonie. " Mark had to come this way on business and his sister asked him to bring some photographs for me to see or I don't suppose he would have bothered to come and see me. I was godmother to his sister's little girl."

Leonie had the snaps in her bag and she fetched them out to show Fran.

" Doesn't Mark regret the broken engagement?"

" Apparently not. He went abroad almost immediately after the quarrel and I have only seen him once at his sister's home since then, apart from his visit here yesterday. I know he has had a house built and he told me it was waiting for his wife. Before he went to America he was buying a house for us which we chose together. I suppose he sold it when the wedding was called off and I believe the one he has had built is a much nicer house. He is in a much better position now than he was when we were engaged."

They had to stop talking to attend to customers. It was strange that when they were in the shop during the slack times they would hang about waiting for customers, but today, because the shop had not been open several came in and complained that they had been before but there was no one there.

When the customers left it was time for Fran to go. " Are you working on any more stories?" asked Leonie.

" Oh, yes," said Fran. " As fast as I finish one I start another, or I start revising one or two that have been returned. An editor will sometimes make a suggestion for improving the story when he returns it and I always try to carry out his instructions. I spend a fortune in postage stamps you know, for everyone has to have the return postage enclosed."

" I suppose you are dying to get back to your typewriter so I won't keep you," smiled Leonie. " Sorry I kept you outside in the cold so long."

When Fran had gone she told herself it would be a good idea if she took her with her on her trip round the world for then Fran would have plenty to write about. But she couldn't leave Angela all alone. There was always someone to consider.

Leonie was surprised that Justin didn't come to the shop. She guessed he was working on the sketches he had made yesterday. He said he had been longing to start on them, making them into oil paintings, but he could have mentioned that he wouldn't be coming in.

She tried to interest herself in a paperback she was half-way through but her mind kept straying. She looked up to see a man entering the shop and then rose to her feet quickly. It was Mark. Her face lit up. " Mark! I thought you would be nearly home by now."

" You didn't think I'd go without saying good-bye, did you?" he said. " I had to thank you for a pleasant evening. I'm afraid I was a bit rude nearly going off to sleep at your friend's home. Will you apologize to them for me?"

" They understood that you had done a lot of travelling and were very tired. You aren't going to start for home at this time in the day, are you?"

" It is late, isn't it?" he said. " I'm afraid I slept rather late, and then I got talking to some fellows in the hotel."

She thought he still looked rather tired. " I shouldn't go back today," she said.

" You started back from our place later than this," he reminded her.

" Yes, but it was light nights then," she said, " and not so unpleasant to drive late at night."

105

" I might as well get off," he said. " I've paid my bill at the hotel."

" You could stay overnight at the bungalow," she told him. " We can put you up quite comfortably."

He hesitated and then he said. " Would you really like me to?"

" Of course. I wouldn't ask you if I didn't want you to stay."

" Where's Justin?" he asked.

" He's working on those sketches. He is going to do them in oils."

" Does he sell them?"

" He does quite well, actually. During the summer he sketches portraits and this summer he has been kept busy most of the time. He earns quite a lot, I think I told you. And then he likes to do landscapes and pictures of the sea. He's very good and gets good prices for those. But I think his sketches of people are the best."

Mark began to laugh. " The only thing I ever did good at art was the painting of an apple. I remember it was pinned up on the wall and I was very proud of it."

Leonie laughed. " Well that's better than I did. I never had anything pinned on the wall. All I got was sarcastic comments from the arts teacher."

" If I'd been behind him I'd have punched his nose," he said, still laughing.

Leonie thought it was strange he should say that. He would protect her from someone else's sarcasm, but he was more often than not sarcastic towards her himself.

" Had you better ring through and ask them if it's all right for me to stay overnight at your place?" he asked.

Her heart leapt for joy. He was accepting her invitation to stay. " I can't," she said, " we aren't on the phone at the bungalow. But it will be all right, I know. Will you watch the shop while I go down to the kitchen and make some coffee? Just give me a call if someone comes though I'm not

106

rushed at the moment. You should see this shop in the summer. It gets packed."

" You wouldn't like to give it up?"

" I have been thinking about it," she said, over her shoulder as she went down the steps to the kitchen.

He followed her down and looked around. " Nice and cosy," he said. " I suppose you and Justin spend a lot of time down here."

" No we don't," she snapped. " We're usually too busy."

He stood looking at her for a moment and then turned to go back up the narrow steps. When she had made the coffee and went back into the shop with a tray she saw that he was looking around the shop examining all the items she had for sale.

He put down the toy jack-in-the-box he had been playing with when he saw her and he relieved her for the tray. " Where?" he asked.

" Here," she said, indicating a space on the counter she was making.

She poured the coffee and as she handed him a cup their hands touched and it was as if an electric current ran from him to her. She wondered if he felt it too, but he said nothing. He walked over to the window and stood looking out across to the sea as he drank his coffee.

She was able to feast her eyes on him while he had his back to her. When he handed her his empty cup she said, " Would you like another?"

His eyes met hers and he said, " I'd love one if there's another going. You always made a good cup of coffee, just how I like it."

" Have you had a midday meal?" she asked, as she poured him another cup.

" No," he said. " I thought I'd be on my way before midday, but I got talking, as I told you. I never thought about a meal, as a matter of fact."

" Well, mum will have something good ready for when

107

we get in. She always has something nice for me when I get home, and I'm sure she'll be able to squeeze a little extra out for you."

She handed him his coffee taking care not to touch his hand this time. It was most disturbing when their hands touched and she didn't want to make it obvious that she still cared for him. It might embarrass him.

" I'll shut the shop as soon as I've washed the cups," she said, " and then we can get off and tell mum and my aunt that you're stopping."

Mark was studying the *hors d'oeuvre* dish in cut glass. " I'll buy that for my mother," he said.

" Oh, it's very expensive," she said.

" I don't begrudge a few pounds for a present for mother," he smiled. " How much is it?"

Leonie quoted a price which was much less than the retail price. " I'll take that," he said.

" I'll wrap it when I've put these away," she said, going off to wash them up.

When she returned he had chosen a present for Paula too. It was a pretty little box ornamented with shells. " I'll take this too," he said, " and if you don't mind I'll pay the correct price. You reduced the price for this by almost half," he said, pointing to the price tag.

" But it's for your mother," she said, her face colouring.

" Is that why you reduced it? I thought you were inefficient and I wondered how you made your shop pay if you made mistakes like that."

" I'm not so stupid as you think," she snapped. " I knew very well what I should have charged a stranger, but I couldn't take that much from you."

He put the items back. " In that case I won't have them," he teased.

" Please let me give you a discount," she said. " I make a lot of profit on those."

" All right. Five per cent only," he smiled.

She wrapped them for him and he handed her the cash. " The best sale I've had today," she beamed at him.

" I'm glad I called then," he said.

Leonie was glad too. Not because he had bought something from her, but because it was nice to think he wouldn't leave without saying good-bye, and also he was being rather nice today.

She locked up the shop and they went running to his car. He put his arm around her, " To keep you warm," he said. " This wind is biting."

" It was different a few weeks ago," she said. " We've had a lovely summer."

" I'm glad for you," he said, and she had the feeling he was not referring to the weather.

It didn't take long to get to the bungalow in his car. Mark was a speedy driver. They could smell the delicious aroma of cooking as soon as they went through the back door. " Mum," called Leonie. " I've bought someone with me who's starving."

" Oh, is that Justin then?" her mother called back, and Leonie looked at Mark in confusion. He would be thinking Justin was always at the bungalow and draw only one conclusion.

" No, it's Mark," she said. " He hasn't started back after all."

Her mother came into the kitchen and gave Mark a welcoming smile. " Hello there, Leonie thought you'd set off early this morning."

" I've told Mark we can put him up, Mum, that's all right, isn't it?"

" Of course it is. We shall be delighted to have you stay with us for as long as you're down here, Mark."

" Thanks," he said. " It's not much pleasure being on your own in a hotel amongst strangers, though I ought to be used to it by now, for I have to travel for my firm and often have to stay out of town for a night."

" There's no need to do that when you come to Cornwall,"
said Mrs. Drew. " We're only too pleased to accommodate
you."

" You might not be after he's eaten tonight," laughed
Leonie. " He hasn't had a midday meal."

" Neither have you I'll bet," said her mother, " and hardly
any breakfast either. A tiny bit of toast. I don't know what's
the matter with you."

Mark looked at Leonie, keenly, and her colour rose once
again. Would he guess that pining for him made her lose
her appetite?

Mrs. Drew turned to Mark. " I'm glad you're hungry,
we've got your favourite roast beef and Yorkshire pudding."

" Fancy you remembering that's my favourite," he smiled,
looking very pleased.

" Go along into the sitting-room and I'll call you when
it's ready. It won't be long. Aunt Louise has made some of
her special pastries too, and there's plenty for us all."

They went through into the other room and when Leonie
saw that Mark was comfortably seated she went off to change
herself. Her stomach felt all churned up with excitement at
having Mark here like this. Just as it used to be when they
were engaged. He had always been fond of her mother, and
she of him. She knew it was silly to get excited because she
had him for a little longer near to her, but she couldn't help
it.

In no time she was out of the jumper and jeans and
changed into a pale blue dress with a pleated skirt. It was
almost new and she felt it suited her slim figure. She gave
herself a spray of perfume, brushed her hair until it shone
like silk and satisfied she had made herself look as nice as
she could went casually into the sitting-room trying to look
as if she hadn't been persevering like mad to make herself
look beautiful.

As she went past his chair he reached out for her hand
and gave it a squeeze. They looked into each other's eyes and

110

it seemed they were discovering each other all over again. She felt shy, as she'd done when she first went out with him. Was he remembering that first time he had reached out for her hand as he was doing now? It had been at one of Paula's parties. She had known him, slightly, catching a glimpse of him occasionally for she had been friendly with Paula for years. But he was older than Paula and usually out when Leonie called round. But at this party it seemed the first time they had really seen each other properly, and they had fallen in love. They knew before the evening was out that they were going to be really special to each other. Paula had been delighted. " I never dreamt that I should have you for my sister-in-law," she said. " It's wonderful."

When Leonie was twenty-one they arranged for their wedding to take place before the summer ended. Mark had a good job at that time though not as good as he had today. They had spent weeks house hunting and at last found a nice semi-detached which suited Mark's pocket and he'd put a deposit on it right away. They had spent all their available spare time looking at furniture and Leonie had known exactly how she was going to furnish their house, the colour of the curtains, and the colour scheme of her kitchen, the bathroom and so forth. She couldn't wait for the wedding day. And then Mark had dropped that bombshell. The wedding was to be postponed. He was going to America. He hadn't even discussed it with her, pointed out the advantages, asked her if she minded, just told her he was going and given her no time to realize that it would be a good thing for their future and that he couldn't afford not to go. It had all been arranged when she was told about it and he was on his way within a few hours of breaking the news to her that he was going.

And how foolish she had been to tell him she could marry Eliot tomorrow if she wished. She had never been all that interested in Eliot, ever. It had just been to make Mark jealous, to stop him going away and leaving her, and her stupidity had caused her to lose him altogether.

He held her hand as they went into the dining-room when her mother called to them that the meal was ready. It was just heavenly to feel her fingers entwined in his. Was he simply showing his gratitude to her because she had saved him a long dreary journey in the dark?

She saw her mother's eyes linger on their hands before she pointed out to Mark where he was to sit. She knew her mother wouldn't make any comments, nor would Aunt Louise. They were souls of discretion.

Mark did justice to the meal they put before him and that was the surest way of winning their approval. The beef was beautifully cooked, luscious and tender, and Aunt Louise made wonderful Yorkshire pudding.

"You know," said Mark, popping more meat into his mouth, "you can stay in the most luxurious hotels and not get a meal served as good as this. I've often heard my colleagues praising a meal and it makes me wonder what sort of meals they have at home if they can praise inferior cooked food."

"It always grieves me to see young people going out spending so much money on meals as they do when we could feed a large family on what they charge one person," said Mrs. Drew.

"People like the atmosphere of eating out," said Leonie. "It makes a change from always eating at home, and expenses are high because wages are high these days."

They sat talking over the meal, Mark declaring he'd eaten far too much, but he couldn't resist those wonderful pastries and fresh cream.

"Move into the lounge now," said Leonie's mother, "while we clear up."

"We couldn't let you wash up after doing all that cooking," said Mark. "Leonie and I will do it."

They could see that he meant it and so they went to take their ease while Leonie and Mark washed up, "I think I shall have to loosen my belt first," he laughed. " I must have put on a stone."

Leonie started the hot water flowing into the bowl and squeezed in the soap liquid while Mark watched her making her feel very self conscious. She turned her head and saw the expression in his eyes that made her pulses race. She had to look away just in case she was making a mistake and that it was not love she saw in his expression. It was wishful thinking, surely. She began to busily collect the dishes and start washing up in a business-like manner.

She switched on the portable radio and the music filled the kitchen. He didn't speak and she wondered if he thought she'd put it on to stop him saying anything when, in fact, it was because it stopped her having to think of something to say.

Suddenly they heard the boom calling the lifeboat. Mark looked at her startled, " What was that?" he asked, as another boom was heard.

" A call for the lifeboat," she said. " It goes out most days on some errand or other. I suppose it's rough out on the sea tonight, it has looked angry all day."

" Can we go out and watch it go?" he asked. " I've never seen a lifeboat go out."

" Of course, if we go in your car we'll be in time to see them launch it."

She called out to her mum that they were going out to see the lifeboat and they picked up their coats and ran to the car. Leonie found herself repeating to Mark some of the stories Justin had told her about the lifeboat men who all gave their services, often their lives, quite voluntarily.

She had seen the boat go out many times and yet it always gave her a thrill of pride to see the brave men go out on to the rough seas. To Mark it was even more fascinating and he moved to the front to see all that went on.

" When the holidaymakers are here there are crowds to watch as they go out," said Leonie.

113

" I'm not surprised," said Mark. " It's quite an impressive sight."

He moved forward and got talking to men standing around to try and discover why the lifeboat had been called.

" There's a fellow been taken ill on one of the trawlers," an old fisherman told him. " They've gone to fetch him in."

" I wouldn't like to be out there fishing tonight," said Mark.

" Oh, I've seen much worse seas than that," said the old man, dismissing the unruly waves quite casually.

These men of the seas just loved to talk to people like Mark about their experiences and soon he was listening in fascination to stories of shipwrecks, and wonderful feats of bravery.

" We've had some miraculous escapes in my time," he said, and went on to tell how he had been saved when a lifeboat had been dashed on the rocks many years ago. Many men lost their lives that night, and he was lucky to be alive to tell the story.

They stood listening until Mark could feel Leonie shivering with cold. " Come on," he said, " or you'll be catching your death," and they were glad to get into the warm car.

" I'm glad I've seen the lifeboat go out," he said, " and I hope they get that poor chap to hospital in time."

" So do I," said Leonie, and as he started the car she said, " I'll bet mum's finished the washing up for us by now."

" Oh, gosh, I forgot that," he said, and speeded the car on its way back to the bungalow.

When they got out of the car he put his arm round her, pulled her close to him and kissed her on the cheek before they went indoors. Her face was rosy with pleasure and she was sure her mother and aunt, who were finishing off the washing up, must have noticed.

EIGHT

" The wind has made you look nice and rosy," said Leonie's mother. " It smells cold outside. There's a nice warm fire in the lounge."

" You should have left that washing up," said Mark. " We would have done it."

" It's done now, don't worry," said Aunt Louise, hanging up the towel.

Leonie and Mark took off their coats and went into the warmth. " Would you like some music?" asked Leonie.

" It depends," he said. " Do you still like the same as I do?"

" I think so," she answered, " unless your taste has changed."

She found a tape of Spanish music which Mark had bought for her just before they were engaged. She hadn't played it for a long time for it bought back memories of happier days and made her feel depressed. Perhaps it would look too obvious if she played that first, so she put on some other numbers, more modern.

Very conscious of Mark sitting behind her as she sorted through the tapes she tried to hide her excitement and kept her eyes down, making a pretence of studying carefully the next tape to put on.

He was sitting on the settee and she would have loved to sit beside him and rest her head on his shoulder but didn't want to appear too pushing so busied herself doing nothing. " Would you like a drink?" she asked.

" Yes, please," he said, smiling at her lazily.

115

" Whisky?"

" Please."

She slopped some into the glass feeling all nerves and he laughed. " Good gracious, woman, do you intend to get me drunk!" He held up the glass to let her see the generous amount she had poured for him.

" It's better than being skinny," she retorted, as she poured herself a sherry.

" You're skinnier than you used to be," he said. " How heavy are you these days?"

" About seven stones I think. I haven't weighed myself for ages."

He pulled her down beside him and put his arm around her waist. " See, nothing to hold," he laughed.

" Well at least I don't have to diet," she said.

" I thought you were dieting. Your mother said you didn't have a midday meal, and hardly any breakfast."

" But I made up for it when I came in tonight," she laughed. " I can eat what I like and I don't get fat."

" You must be worrying over something. Are you, Leonie?"

" Not really," she answered, soberly.

" Are you sure? The shop paying well?"

" Exceeding all expectations. I told you Justin brings in a lot of customers."

" But didn't I hear you say in the shop you had given some thought to giving it up."

" I have considered it," she said. " I thought I would like to travel."

" Is that your own idea?"

" Yes," she said. " You ask a lot of questions about me, but what about you?"

" What do you want to know about me?"

" When are you getting married?"

" Who said I was getting married?"

" You did."

" When did I say that?"

" You told me your house was just waiting for your wife."

" Oh, of course."

" Will the wedding be soon?"

" I'd like it to be."

She turned away from him and began to choose the next tape for the present one was nearly finishing. She took out the Spanish one. Why not remind him of what they had once meant to each other?

She waited for the tape to finish and then changed it and waited for his reaction. For a moment it didn't seem to have any effect, but at last he looked up at her from the settee. " Ah, I remember that," he said. He rose slowly and with his hands on her hips began to sway with her to the music. It was gay music and it was quite easy for them to get carried away by the rhythm. They were laughing into each other's eyes, then their mood changed and they became serious. He responded to the longing in hers and gathered her up into his arms. Her heart was pumping away like mad.

" Oh, Leonie, darling," he said, his mouth against her face.

" Mark," she breathed. " Oh, Mark."

His mouth found hers and she was filled with such joy. She clung to him returning kiss for kiss. It was unbelievably wonderful to be back in his arms after all this time. They could only murmur each other's names, words were superfluous. But they were brought back to earth by the sound of a car arriving and the slamming of a car door. She drew away from him. " That must be Justin," she said.

Mark's look changed to one of contempt as he pushed her away from him. The door bell rang and he said, bitterly. " Saved by the bell. I'm afraid I allowed myself to be carried away."

He mistook the reason for the distress in her eyes and said, " Don't worry, Leonie. I won't tell him what a two-timing little cheat you are. You've been leading me on ever since I came here and yet you knew he was coming round for you."

There was no time for her to deny that for her mother entered looking a little anxious. "Justin," she announced.

"Hello, Justin," said Mark, in a casual voice. It was plain to Leonie that he had not been affected by their kisses as she had been for he was quite calm while her pulses were still racing. "What's the weather like outside, I was just thinking of going down to the front to see if the lifeboat had returned."

"It's not bad in the car," said Justin.

Mark went for his car coat and as he shrugged into it he said, "Cheerio, I'll be seeing you."

Mrs. Drew looked after him with a worried expression and then she left Leonie alone with Justin.

"I thought he was leaving right away?" said Justin.

"Yes, he intended to," said Leonie, hardly able to bring herself to speak to Justin she was so annoyed at his untimely arrival. "He paid his bill at the hotel but got delayed talking to one and another until it seemed late to start on such a long journey so I suggested he stayed here. It's not pleasant driving all that way in the dark."

He looked at her keenly and seeing her unhappy expression was convinced that nothing had developed between herself and Mark in his absence. She went and stopped the tape and he said, "I like that, you should have left it on."

"I've got a bit of a headache," she lied.

"Oh, I'm sorry. Well I haven't come to stop, love. I thought I ought to come and explain why I didn't come to the shop today. The time has been flying for me too. I became so engrossed in my painting that I never noticed the time all day. I had to tear myself away to come and see you in case you were worried about what happened to me," he added, wryly.

"There was no need for you to leave your work on my

118

account," she told him. "I guessed you were working and I understand. You wanted to get cracking right away, yesterday, didn't you?"

"Yes, but I would hate to think I was neglecting you."

"You don't have to consider me," she said.

He put his arm around her and she felt she would scream. She couldn't stand it after being in Mark's arms.

"But I do consider you, princess," he said, and she could have shuddered at his use of that word. It had never annoyed her until Mark had made fun of it.

"Would you like a drink?" she asked, seeing his eyes rest on the whisky in the glass which Mark hadn't finished.

"No, thanks, Leonie. I can see you're not yourself. I'll let you get off to bed early if you've got a headache."

With an effort she gave him a smile. "I suppose you are anxious to get back to your painting, anyway."

"Yes. But I couldn't go through a day without seeing you. I wish we were married, Leonie, and then you'd be close to me all the time and even though I was working it would be nice to know you were there."

He left shortly afterwards and Leonie took herself off to bed. She felt she couldn't face Mark after he had called her a two-timing cheat.

She lay in bed waiting for him to return. It wasn't too late, he was probably being considerate in returning early as he was staying in someone else's home. She heard a little chattering in the kitchen, and then everything was quiet and she guessed everyone was in bed.

It was an endless night. Suppose she went into Mark and told him how she felt. She was not a cheat, she loved him, and Justin knew she did. And if it came to that, what about himself? He had told her he hoped to get married soon, and yet he had kissed her like that. What would Josy, if it was Josy he was going to marry, have thought of that?

Mark was up early the next morning. She heard him talking to her mother, and going backwards and forwards to

119

his car. She watched from her window. He was obviously putting in all his belongings so he was going. Listlessly she got dressed and prepared herself to see him for the last time.

He was alone in the dining-room when she went in and he looked up to see her unhappy expression. "Cheer up, Leonie," he said. "I was as bad as you last night. Let's forget all about it."

She nearly cried out that she didn't want to forget all about it. It had been heavenly being held in his arms. Why was he so blind? Or didn't he care? That was it. He didn't care for her any more, or he would have known how she felt.

"I see you've been putting your things in the car," she said, coolly. "Leaving then?"

"Might as well," he said, with a shrug. "As you say it isn't exactly holiday weather. I might come down when the weather's nice and perhaps you'll be married then to your wonderful prince."

"Don't, Mark," she begged. "I hate you when you're sarcastic."

"Don't tell me you love me when I'm not."

She gave him a look of appeal. Couldn't he see how much she did love him.

Her mother entered with a piled up breakfast for him. "You don't know what time it will be before you get another meal," she said, "so I've put you plenty. What about you, Leonie, ready for yours?"

"No, I don't want any," said Leonie.

Mark looked at her, but made no comment. He managed to eat all that her mother had put before him so his appetite was not impaired.

He was ready to go before she set out for the shop and as he was about to get into his car he said, "I'll give your love to Mother and to Paula, Leonie."

"And to little Samantha," she added.

120

Almost as an afterthought he turned to put his arm around Leonie and he gave her a kiss. " 'Bye, Leonie," he said. " I like your Justin. He'll be good to you. Perhaps he loves you more than I did."

He thanked her mother for her hospitality and she told him he was welcome to stay whenever he wished. Leonie watched him go quite calmly. She felt dead inside.

She walked round the streets for ages before going to the shop that day. She was not shedding any tears but felt she was crying deep within herself. How stupid to want one person with all one's being as she did. She wondered if there were other people as stupid as herself breaking her heart over a man after two years of breaking off her engagement to him. She had had plenty of time to get over him, and yet she felt she could crawl into a corner and die out of her misery.

She didn't know why she didn't hate him for hadn't he made her feel cheap last night? He said she had been leading him on when in fact she had been most careful not to let him think she was throwing herself at him. It had been he who had made the advances, except perhaps when she had kissed him when they were dancing. She might have asked for that for she had been dying for him to kiss her, and so he did. If he thought she was cheap what did he think about girls who went to bed with fellows whether they loved them or not?

In the shop she began to clear up the kitchen, scrubbing down the shelves and cleaning out the cupboards. It didn't really want doing but she had to do something to keep her mind occupied away from Mark.

It was lonely without Justin, but this morning she didn't feel she wanted to see anyone. It was lunch time when he came. This was the morning Fran didn't come and he said, " I've bought you something to eat. Have you had anything?"

" No," she said, " what have you bought?"

" Cornish pasties."

121

" It's a wonder you don't look like one," she said, " you really ought to have proper meals, Justin."

" Do you want to take me in hand?" he grinned.

" Someone ought to," she said.

" Headache gone?" he asked.

" Yes, thanks."

" You still look very peaky. Has Mark gone?"

" Yes." She didn't want to talk about Mark to Justin at the moment and said, " How's your painting coming on?"

" Not so bad. You always feel you could do better," he said.

" I'll make some coffee. We'll go into the kitchen, shall we? I don't suppose we'll be bothered very much while we have something to eat."

" Right," he said. " Let me go and make the coffee and I'll call you when it's ready."

When she went down to him he said, " You've been having a bit of a spring clean, haven't you? I couldn't find anything."

Although Leonie had eaten no breakfast she could only pick at the Cornish pasty. She cut it in half knowing she wouldn't eat it all.

" You can have half of mine," she said, " you look as if you're enjoying that. When did you last have a cooked meal?"

" When I'm engrossed in my work I'm not bothered about food," he told her.

They ate in silence for a bit. Justin kept looking at her seriously and she knew he would have liked to know what happened between herself and Mark but he didn't ask.

He ate every bit of her Cornish pasty as well as his own and had another cup of coffee, then as he was putting the cups to be washed, and she came to do them he caught her in his arms. " What's the matter, love? You look as if you are choked up."

His kindness brought the tears that had not come earlier.

She let him hold her close and she stifled her sobs against his chest. " I thought everything was going to be all right last night," she said. " Mark and I had been to see the life-boat go out and he was lovely to me. When we came back I put on that tape which he had bought for me, the one you said you liked when you came in, and it brought back memories for him as well as for me. We danced, and then he kissed me and I felt sure he loved me; he made me think he loved me. But then you came and he was vile. He accused me of being a cheap little two-timer. He went off, as you know, and this morning he left early. He wished you and me every happiness, and said you probably loved me more than he used to. He put it in the past tense to let me know he doesn't love me now."

Justin held her without attempting to kiss her and comfort her that way and she was thankful, she'd had enough of kisses. She felt she never wanted to be kissed by anyone again.

" Do you think I messed something up for you by coming round last night?" he asked.

" No. He said he had been saved by the bell. He let me know that he had allowed himself to be carried away by the music when we danced and that it didn't mean anything to him at all."

When she had recovered her self-control she said, " Justin, I'm going to sell the shop."

" Do you think that's wise?" he asked. " You need some-thing to help you take your mind off your personal problems, surely."

" I want to get away," she said. " It isn't really fair to you, Justin, to go on seeing you knowing I have nothing to offer you. See how I take advantage of you—crying on your shoulder."

" I'd sooner you cried on my shoulder than anyone else's," he said, and pulled her closer still.

" But I've made up my mind," she said, pulling away
123

from him. "I've talked it over with my mother and aunt. They think they might buy it from me."

"But what will you do?" he asked, in consternation.

"I'm going to travel round the world."

"What! On your own?" His expression made her laugh.

"My cousin from Australia has done it twice," she informed him.

"But you don't seem the type, Leonie. You'd have to rough it a lot of the way."

"It's the only way I can think of to forget myself. I shall be struggling for survival I expect and it will strengthen my character."

"If you're going round the world I'm coming with you," he said.

"No, you're not," she replied. "The idea is to go away so that you will forget me and fall in love with someone else."

"Well you should know that that's easier said than done, shouldn't you?"

"I would have been over Mark by now if I hadn't seen him twice this year. When I see him I start longing for him more. I must go away on my own."

"All round the world on your own? Oh, Leonie!" he laughed.

She looked back at him and laughed too at the expression in his eyes. "You don't think I can do it?"

"I'd be very surprised. Just think about it. Where would you start?"

"From here," she said, and laughed again.

"There are some tidy characters in the world today," he said. "You'd come across them all. You're just the type to be taken in by all the crooks and scoundrels."

She thought about all the stories she had heard about white slave trafficking and the awful things that had happened to girls travelling abroad on their own and suddenly had cold feet.

" I think I'd better marry you instead, Justin," she giggled.

" That's twice you've proposed to me," he grinned. " I could have taken advantage of you, you see. I'll take you round the world, Leonie, with no strings attached."

" And do you think when I come back I will have forgotten all about Mark and be in love with you?"

" It's a possibility, isn't it?"

" Mark said he liked you, and I do, very much."

" Did you talk to Mark as you do to me? You pour your heart out to me and I know all about you. Does Mark?"

" He used to. But he doesn't know how I feel now."

" You're a funny kid. You've told me over and over again that you don't love me. You don't mind saying that to me at all so why should you be wary of telling a man that you do?"

" It would embarrass him."

" Just think how marvellous it would be for him if he wanted you to be in love with him. A man would rather hear a girl tell him she loves him than that she doesn't. It doesn't do anything for his ego at all to say you only like him."

" I love you, Justin," she said. " I really do, you know that. But I'm not in love with you."

" I think you should have been just as candid with Mark. You should have told him you still loved him and wanted that ring back if he was still keeping it for you."

" If he made me feel that he loved me, told me over and over again that he did, as you do, it would be so easy to do that," she sighed. " There's someone who does love you, Justin, and you deserve to be loved."

" Someone who loves me?"

" Don't say you aren't aware of the fact. Men really are the limit. The poor girl runs after you waiting on you hand and foot and you don't even know she's head over heels in love with you."

" You mean little Fran," he said, slowly.

" Yes, isn't it obvious to you?"

125

" I hope it's just a young girl's crush and she'll grow out of it."

" You see, you're not pleased to know that she loves you. You would rather she didn't."

" It's flattering, but I wish it weren't true."

" I rather feel I shouldn't have told you," said Leonie. " Fran would die if she knew I was talking like this. You won't ever let her know I've told you, will you?"

" It's best that I should know. I'll be careful not to hurt her. And you see, Leonie, I'm not treating it lightly, or feeling embarrassed about it, and if anything, I feel fonder than ever of Fran."

" But supposing she had told you about her love herself? How would you have felt? And how would she have felt when you had to let her know her love wasn't returned?"

" No worse than she does now," said Justin. " I wouldn't ridicule her or anything to make her feel wretched. Fran knows that I love you, anyway, so she's not expecting me to return her love."

" And I know that Mark is in love and will be married soon, at least he hopes to be, for he told me so."

" Do you mean to tell me you let him kiss you and make believe he thought a lot of you when he's told you he is going to marry someone else?"

" Yes. I was mad, wasn't I? He was only playing with me and I was stupid enough to take it seriously. No wonder he thought I was cheap."

" He told you that when I arrived on the scene?"

" Yes," said Leonie, and Justin looked at her strangely.

They went back into the shop and Justin noticed that the display of fine ware had been depleted. " I see you've been having some good sales," he said.

" Mark bought the cut-glass *hors d'oeuvre* dish for his mother," said Leonie. " You know, Justin, it's rather nice selling better class gifts. Makes you feel you are in a higher class trade altogether."

" Apart from that, if you sell one pricy gift the profit is as much on that as on two or three dozen of the small items. You get a higher turnover for less work."

" Yes. You should be in business, Justin."

" No, thanks. I have no inclination at all to make a lot of money, love. I just enjoy my life as it is. My father spent a lifetime making a fortune."

" And he just had to die and leave it," said Leonie. " I suppose that's how I feel in a way. That's why I suddenly wanted to get rid of the shop. It takes up all my time and I don't feel that I'm really living."

He was quiet for a long time, and then he said. " I don't know how to advise you, Leonie. If you are not happy in England you are not likely to be happy in any other country. Happiness is inside you, not to be found in any particular part of the world."

" I know it's no good going in search of happiness, Justin. I just thought if I travelled and had to rough it as my cousin has done that it would bring me to my senses. Make me grow up, so to speak. I would have no time for nonsense."

She paused for a time and then she looked at him, smiling a little. " I think it's all talk, Justin. I'm sure I haven't the courage to go travelling all alone. I have some money, more than Caroline set out with, so I wouldn't have to rough it that much, but I don't think I could cope."

" It will take you some time to have the shop turned over to your mother and your aunt if they want to buy it from you, and you'd have to see them settled in. Fran would be a good help to them, it was a good thing you asked her to come in part-time, she's picked up the job nicely, and would be a godsend to newcomers in the shop until they'd got the hang of it. I've got one or two things to attend to myself. If you are absolutely sure you want to sell the shop, go ahead, and then I'll plan this trip for you, and come with you. Just as a watchdog."

" As a good friend," she said. " I think I might end up falling for you after all, Justin."

" It would be the answer to my prayers," he smiled. " I'm going to love and leave you now. I shall be busy for the next few days so if I don't come into the shop don't start thinking I've run off, or I've died of starvation, will you?"

" No, I won't. I feel better for talking to you."

After he'd gone she began to think about what she was letting herself in for, taking a trip to so many countries with Justin. It was just the opposite of what she had intended. The idea of selling up was to leave him so that he could find himself another girl, but instead, if he travelled for weeks with her they would become even more close than they were at the present time.

Would that be so bad? He was willing to accompany her with no strings attached, hadn't he said so? Her musings had to stop for a young boy and his sister came in to buy a present for their mother's birthday and they were ages making up their minds. They had only a few shillings between them and Leonie wanted them to choose something that would be appreciated by their mother.

The little girl wanted to buy a birthday book because it had a pretty cover, but Leonie couldn't imagine their mother being too thrilled with that. The boy wanted perfume and eventually they agreed on that and Leonie had to reduce the price of the bottle they chose for they hadn't sufficient to pay for it. But she had the satisfaction of seeing two happy children going out of the shop. " Don't tell anyone I reduced the price," she said, for she had done favours like that before only to have the children return with their friends expecting the same favours.

The day passed with a trickle of customers here and there to pass the time. Some of them were local people she had got to know and they stopped to chat with her. She thought it would have been a good thing for Fran to have been with her for she heard several stories about family problems which would have given Fran ideas for her short stories. The only thing was that the stories were so unusual that readers would think the author had exaggerated half the time. Truth was certainly stranger than fiction, Leonie decided.

She was lucky to have been accepted as a friend by many of the Cornish people who were not over eager to make friends with people from other parts of the country, regarding them as foreigners with no right to come and settle in Cornwall.

She closed early and strolled home leisurely. What was she going to do with her evenings now that there was no longer any reason to keep open late for the tourists? Justin had told her he wouldn't be seeing her for the next few days so she would have to try to amuse herself. She would have called round to see Fran and Angela, but if they wanted to devote their time to writing it wasn't fair to go and take up their time.

It had been so long since she had had time to spare away from the shop that she hardly knew how to spend it. She supposed her mother and aunt would be glad of more of her company, for they didn't see much of her though she lived with them.

It hardly seemed any time at all since she had been coming down to the front with Mark to see the lifeboat go out. He had been so fascinated with it all and with the old fisherman who had told him so many tales. Mark would be home by now, she thought. All the time she had been in the shop today he had been speeding away from her. Back to the girl he intended to marry. The one who would be lucky enough to share that lovely house he had had built since he had been made a director of his firm.

She had to forget him. She would see that she was never in his company again. If Paula invited her to her home she would make an excuse not to go. In future it would be better to make herself believe that a man named Mark True-man no longer existed as far as she was concerned. If she didn't make herself forget her life was never going to be worth living. From now on she would make plans which did not include marriage. She could understand girls who wouldn't tie themselves to a man. If things went wrong the heartache was too great. She almost wished she had never met Mark, but if she hadn't she would never have known what love was.

NINE

Leonie was surprised at the enthusiasm her mother and Aunt Louise developed over the taking over of her gift shop. They had apparently talked it over very thoroughly and decided they would like to run it though they knew they would have to get someone to help them during the summer months. Helping Leonie occasionally when she was busy was different to running the shop entirely themselves, but they said they were looking forward to it if Leonie was sure she wanted to give it up.

They had gone thoroughly into the question of finance. It would take all their savings to buy the shop from Leonie for it was a much better shop now than when Leonie had bought it at a low price because it had been neglected. Leonie had ploughed a lot of her profits back into the shop so that it was now a well-stocked thriving business.

Leonie was not anxious to make a lot of money out of the deal, nor was she requiring all the money at once. " If you take it over you can pay for the shop out of your profits to save using up all your capital," she told them.

" Well perhaps we should keep some money in hand for buying stock," said her mother. " Your auntie and I know that there is a slack period ahead for the shop, but it's nearing Christmas and soon afterwards, by the time we have really got the hang of running it there will be the early spring tourists to get us slowly warmed up before we are faced with the terrific summer trade. We would gradually get into it instead of being plunged head first right at the busiest time.

131

I've told your auntie I shall learn to drive so that I can go to the warehouses when necessary as you do, though I know that most of the warehouses send their representatives to take orders and save a lot of trouble."

" You need to go to the warehouses occasionally to get an idea of the stocks they carry. The representatives can only carry a small proportion."

She told them how satisfied she had been over stocking more expensive items as advised by Justin. " I have had some good sales, even though we are not in the busy season, so it's worth concentrating on the better stuff which carries higher profits."

Leonie felt that if she changed her mind now and decided not to sell the shop her mother and aunt would be most disappointed though it worried her to a certain extent to think that she would be moving on and leaving them the responsibility of the shop, though they might get more pleasure from it than she'd done. For one thing she had taken it as something to take her mind off her broken engagement and the disappointment of not being married as she had hoped to be. But she had not been able to forget Mark.

If Justin decided to travel along with her they would not have him to attract the customers into the shop. She pointed out all the snags and so forth they would encounter but they would not be put off. They were keen to have a go and she had never seen them look so young and sparkling. It seemed they had a new lease of life.

Her mother was talking about starting her driving lessons as soon as possible. " Might as well learn to drive and pass the test, get it over before the place starts swarming with tourists," she said, matter-of-factly.

The thought of all the book-keeping involved held no terrors for them. " Aunt Louise is an excellent book-keeper, she'll cope very well."

It seemed to Leonie that they might well cope better than she did herself, for she had relied on Justin to do her books for her.

"You won't able to keep the bungalow spick and span and do all your lovely cooking if you run a shop," said Leonie.

"We do find it rather boring at times, just cleaning round. We get finished well before dinnertime and we don't know what to do with ourselves sometimes. We seem to find plenty to talk about but think how much more interesting our conversation would be if we had the shop to talk about and plans for making improvements and so on."

"And we'll be of some importance in the town too. We shall get to know many more people and will soon be known as important business people instead of just nobodies."

Leonie laughed with them. They were like excited school-children, and she wished she could get the same enthusiasm for her proposed trip round the world. Perhaps when Justin had the time to make plans with her the excitement would come.

"You will still keep Fran to help you part-time won't you, Mum?" she asked.

"We shall need more than the help she can give us I daresay. Perhaps her friend would be able to help us out as well. We aren't going to overwork ourselves at our time of life and we aren't out to make a fortune, simply to have an interest in life and meet people."

The following day in the shop Leonie told Fran she was planning to give up the shop and Fran's face dropped notice-ably. "You won't lose your job unless you want to," added Leonie, hastily. "My mother and her sister are taking the shop over and they would like you to stay and even sug-gested that Angela might like to help in the busy times too."

But it wasn't the thought of losing her job that was worrying Fran as much as the thought that Justin might move on when new people took over the shop. Leonie felt great sympathy for her. If Justin went with her Fran was

133

going to miss him unbearably, and Leonie knew what heart-break could be.

Of course Fran had never received any encouragement from Justin, had probably known all along that he was in love with Leonie, but it hadn't stopped her loving him. Seeing Fran's face Leonie thought she would prefer to leave Justin behind here to find happiness with Fran rather than take him away with her. But, at the same time, she knew she wouldn't travel very far unless she had company. Leonie was not a loner like her cousin Caroline. She had always required a special friendship with someone. Someone to give affection to. In her early teens it had been Paula she had been very fond of, and still was, and later it had been Mark she loved. To anyone who wanted her affection she had much to give. She was even giving way to Justin in allowing him to accompany her because she knew he loved her, and she knew she would be lost without someone.

" I shall be glad to go on working for your mother," said Fran, practically, " and perhaps Angela will be glad to help too, for it's no use our living in a fool's paradise. We have both worked very hard at our writing since we came to live down here and concentrated all our time and efforts on it, but we have to admit that without the few pounds I get from you, we are receiving very little besides. We paid our rent six months in advance which was one of the conditions made when we took the cottage and the next six months rent has been scraped together. Our parents would be worried to death if they knew how desperate we've been at times."

" And you just have to write?" said Leonie, sympathetically.

" We shall have to give up the idea of ever making a living from writing I'm afraid," said Fran. " Both of us will have to work, and writing will have to be a spare-time occupation."

" Even if Angela's novel is accepted?"

" Even then because she won't know whether it's going

134

to be accepted for ages. If she heard within a month of sending it out she'd be very lucky, and then there are further delays of having to sign a contract. If it is destined to be a best seller it would be ages before she got any royalties because the book wouldn't be published for months and months."

"Oh, dear," said Leonie. "I didn't realize that. Why do you carry on, knowing all the drawbacks?"

"I suppose it's because it is so difficult to make a living at writing. If it was easy it wouldn't be an achievement."

"It's the same with most things," said Leonie. "We all aim for the best and hate to have to do with second best. A runner wants to be a champion, so does a swimmer. Men aim to get to the top of the tree in all walks of life. We must have an aim and you find those at the top have usually more life and perseverance in them than those with no ambition. Perhaps that's why I've lost interest in my shop. At first it was a challenge to see if I could make a good living from it, but now I know that I can there seems little point in carrying on. I want to have a go at something else."

"But what are you going to do now?" asked Fran.

"I haven't decided," said Leonie. She could have told her that she would probably be one of those who had to take second best, which would be what she settled for if she eventually married Justin. She had heard of people who had married a man they didn't love in the beginning and the marriage had been very successful. Perhaps hers would be. She would have to work at it, and that might give her an incentive in life.

"I would like to be married and have a family," she told Fran.

"If I married it would have to be to a man who understood that I wanted to write above everything else," said Fran.

"I hope you find him," said Leonie, and knew that Justin would be the right man for her. He was an artist himself and

135

his art would come first, and he'd surely understand that Fran's writing was just as important to her as his art work was to him. Perhaps she should absolutely refuse to let Justin go away with her. If he stayed in Cornwall seeing Fran regularly he might eventually fall in love with her. They were already good friends.

Leonie knew that Justin was going to be absolutely wrapped up in his work, he had told her not to worry if she didn't see him, but she did expect to have glimpses of him now and again. She missed him calling at lunchtime with a little snack for both of them and sharing her coffee. He had to stop to eat and she fully expected to see him sometime, but there was no sign of him.

She had never been to his place which he shared with a couple of artist friends. Possibly it was always in such a shambles being a bachelor home he had never felt he could take her there, and even if she knew where he was staying she wouldn't intrude. He had told her not to expect to see him, and not to think he was starving himself to death, so she just had to accept that he was too busy to see her, too engrossed in his paintings. If he didn't give himself entirely to his art he would not have been such an excellent artist.

Mrs. Drew had sent for a provisional licence some days ago and when it came she had already arranged to take her first lesson. She dressed herself up for the occasion and Leonie couldn't help realizing that her mother was quite a young person, really. She was forty-seven, which had seemed ancient to Leonie, but now she looked at her with new eyes and saw that she didn't look like a middle-aged woman at all, but was youthful and quite nice-looking. It was a shame that she had been a widow for so long.

When she had taken her first driving lesson she called at the shop and Leonie saw that she was flushed with the exertion and stress of her first lesson, but she had a happy look on her face. She was sure she'd be a driver before very long.

"Why on earth haven't you had a go before?" asked Leonie.

"I've often thought about it," said her mother, "but when I knew I would need to be able to drive to go to warehouses if necessary I was quite excited at the thought of learning. I've been rather stupid in the past, Leonie. I've just accepted a humdrum existence when I could have been out working and making something of my life. I've always excused myself on the grounds that I had to look after you, but I suppose I hadn't the courage and necessary confidence to get a job. Suddenly I've found it and I feel young again, with something to live for."

Leonie looked at her fondly. She admired her courage in starting out afresh and thought that was at least one good thing coming out of her own mess-up. It had given her mother a new interest in life and also her Aunt Louise, who was equally as happy at the thought of being a shopkeeper.

For the past two years Leonie had been so involved in her own unhappiness that she hadn't given a thought to anyone else. She realized how selfishly she had been living, taking it for granted that her mother and her sister were perfectly happy running the home, and because they were good cooks had imagined that that was all they had ever wanted to be. Good housewives. They didn't even have the satisfaction of being wives for both had lost their husbands. It was seeing the sparkle in her mother's eyes after having taken her first driving lesson that made Leonie aware that her mother was still young and could get a lot out of life yet. She could even marry again, and Aunt Louise was only a year or two older. When we are young we are apt to think that people twenty or thirty years older than ourselves are past having an enjoyable existence.

Because she recognized that her mother was still capable of enjoying herself she decided to take her and her Aunt Louise out for a meal that evening. It was true that meals out cost far more than they were worth, but they were worth

137

it in one way because it took people out of themselves into a new atmosphere. Made them think they were with it, and not merely onlookers.

Mrs. Drew hadn't bought anything suitable for evening wear for years, nor had her sister, and they began to look anxiously in their wardrobes to see what they had suitable to wear. When Leonie saw their excitement at the thought of going out in the evening for a meal it came to her even more what a selfish creature she had been, not putting herself out to give them more pleasure.

To Leonie's surprise her mother could quite easily get into one of her own evening gowns. Because her mother had always worn clothes so different from her own she couldn't believe it was possible for her to wear one of her evening gowns and look so good. Aunt Louise had put on a little more weight and so she couldn't struggle into one of Leonie's evening gowns, but Leonie had a full black evening skirt. It was tight round the waist but they found some black material and were able to unpick the band and let some more into it so that with the addition of an inch or two she could get into it, and then she found she had a pretty pink blouse of her own which she could wear with it.

Leonie, who still had her hairdressing skill though she no longer had a salon, shampooed and set their hair for them. This was one of the things she had always done for them— kept their hair nicely styled and set. She made their hairdos a little more sophisticated this evening and then they were ready to go to a place Leonie had often been to with Justin. She had enjoyed getting them ready for a night out, spending more time on them than she did on herself, and felt happier than she'd done for ages. Perhaps that was the secret of happiness, she told herself, living for others instead of oneself. She even began to wonder if there was some sort of work she could do trying to bring happiness to people less fortunate than herself.

" Leonie, who's going to do our hair for us when you

leave us?" wailed her mother.

" Oh, you'll be making so much money in the shop you'll be able to afford to go to the finest hairdressers," said Leonie.

" But you've done my hair for years and know how I like it," she said.

When they went out to the car Leonie said, " We'll get some L plates, Mum, and you'll be able to get some practice with me as well as with your instructor. You'll need all you can get in order to pass the test."

" I've been stupid not to have learned ages ago," said her mother. " I've been silly in lots of ways, and you have Louise. We should have gone out and made new lives for ourselves before now."

" Better late than never," laughed Aunt Louise. " Remember I lost Harry more recently than you lost Fred, I'm only just beginning to realize that I'm free to take up other interests."

Leonie expected them to find fault with the meal and say how much better they could have cooked it, but they were very appreciative of all that was served even wondering how this mushroom sauce was prepared, they hadn't tasted anything like it before. They got through a bottle of wine but refused a second one. " We don't want to become alcoholics," said Mrs. Drew, and Leonie laughed, seeing where her own caution came from. She was always afraid to drink too much in case she became too fond of drinking.

Leonie couldn't get over how young her mother looked wearing her daughter's evening gown. The style didn't look too girlish for her, for the dress was a midnight blue and the cut quite simple. Her mother hadn't a grey hair yet and Leonie felt very proud of her. Aunt Louise too in the pretty shell pink blouse she was wearing with the black skirt looked younger and gayer than Leonie had seen her since she came to Cornwall. She wished she had devoted more of her time to both of them instead of being so full of her own

139

misery, and almost wished she weren't going away now. But perhaps she had launched them on to a new way of life, if nothing else, for her mother said, " We must do this more often Louise, I don't know when I've enjoyed myself so much."

When they arrived back at the bungalow the boom went for the lifeboat, shortly afterwards to be followed by another. They paused before going indoors. "Wonder who's in trouble tonight," said Mrs. Drew, but Leonie was thinking about the last night Mark had been here and they had gone down to the front to see the boat go out. Justin had arrived in time to stop her making a complete fool of herself with Mark for she might easily have told him that she loved him if they had not been disturbed. In fact, if Mark had not been completely carried away himself because he had a girl in his arms, he should have realized that she was in love with him for she had whispered his name over and over again in between kisses. But he had simply believed she was amusing herself the same as he had been, which was as well if he was in love with Josy. But though he himself had been as passionate as Leonie, he had made her feel a wanton afterwards, disregarding his own part in the happening.

She refused to let thoughts of Mark depress her. Her mother and aunt were still talking about their lovely night out and how much they had enjoyed it, and she had been happy herself until she had allowed thoughts of Mark to intrude. She would put him out of her mind, waste no more time on a hopeless love.

And that night she went to sleep immediately her head touched the pillow. In the morning she awoke feeling refreshed and went off to the shop in a happy frame of mind. She felt as if life was good after all, and that there was something wonderful in store for her. Why she should feel like that she didn't know. Perhaps it was because she hadn't seen Justin for a day or so and hadn't been worrying about not being in love with him. It was not very nice to be in a

140

position of having to tell someone you didn't love them, and perhaps that had been making her feel depressed as much as anything.

Later in the morning Mrs. Drew and her sister came to the shop and Leonie sat back and read a library book while they took charge. They were already regarding it as their own shop so she thought she might as well let them take over.

A traveller called with Christmas gifts and Leonie allowed her mother and her aunt to make up their own minds what to stock for Christmas. They were a little vague as to what quantity to order. It was always difficult to assess how much to stock for Christmas but if they ordered gifts that could be sold throughout the year they couldn't go far wrong. Parents spent a lot of money during the holiday period on toys for their children when they were fretful.

The traveller, out to secure a good order for himself, was trying to persuade them to buy large quantities and only then did Leonie intervene to tell her mother not to over-stock. "You can always order more if you sell out before Christmas."

"But our stocks might be finished by then," said the persistent traveller.

"That's a chance we have to take," said Leonie. "It's better for us to sell all our stock and wish we could have had more, than to overstock and wish we had bought less."

The two older ladies made their order, explaining that they were to be the proprietors in future. The traveller looked at Leonie with positive dislike. If she hadn't been present he would have persuaded them to buy a much larger quantity of Christmas ware.

The sisters were quite proud that they had placed their first order and Leonie told them to beware of travellers who were too pushing. "You have the phone here in the shop," she said, " and can always ring for more if you want to. You will soon have a good idea what quantities you need to buy."

141

It had been several days since Leonie had seen Justin and she expected him to come into the shop any time to show her his completed painting. Life had been so uncomplicated for the last day or so she began to think it would be wise if she just went on her way, left without telling Justin, and settled somewhere where he couldn't come and see her. It would give him a chance to forget her, and she would make her own plans for the future.

When Fran arrived she was most disappointed to find Justin had not come to the shop again. " Do you think he's all right?" she asked Leonie. " Would he mind if I went round to see if he is?"

" I don't know," said Leonie. " He told me not to worry if I didn't see him for a time. I've never been round to his place."

" He could be ill and needing someone to look after him."

" He's not living alone, Fran," said Leonie. " He shares with two other artists."

" But they may have left Cornwall while it's quiet."

" I wouldn't think so. It's while it's quiet that they can capture the surrounding scenery and give us such wonderful pictures of the sea when it's turbulent and frightening."

Leonie was sorry for Fran who looked so slim and pale. Life wasn't being too kind to her at the moment. She wasn't having a lot of success with her work or her love life. Leonie had read once that great artists needed to suffer before they could create with any depth and she felt that Fran was certainly suffering at the moment. Perhaps it was all necessary if she was to develop into a writer of any distinction.

In between customers Fran composed poetry and while she wasn't looking Leonie took the liberty of reading some of it and was surprised at the beauty and sincerity in her verses. She didn't even bother to take the poems with her and when Leonie called her to remind her of them she shrugged and said, " You can scrap them. It's impossible to get poetry published these days—no one wants to read it."

Leonie thought that was a great pity for she had enjoyed reading Fran's poetry. She popped the sheets into her handbag. " I'll have them for a keepsake," she told herself. " I'll never destroy them."

Her mother and aunt had left the shop so that they could have a nice meal ready for Leonie when she arrived home. " Who will cook for you when you take over completely?" she asked.

" Oh, we've thought of that," said her aunt. " We shall get someone in to help us at the bungalow, we aren't going to work ourselves to death. We were talking to Mrs. Mason next door and she knows a person who is a wonderful cook though she is getting on a bit in years. She knows she'll be glad to earn an extra pound or two and is arranging for us to meet her."

Leonie had to smile. " You certainly aren't losing any time, are you?" she said. She herself had written by airmail to her cousin Caroline in Australia to ask what route she took back to her own country. " I might be calling to see you some time in the near future," she wrote. She felt that when she'd had a reply to that letter she would be making plans of her own, with or without Justin, and because she felt she was doing something positive was feeling better.

At closing time she counted up the money in the till. It hadn't been a bad day, although they hadn't seemed to have had many customers. The shop didn't make very much out of season, but it wasn't losing money.

She put on her sheepskin-lined coat to walk back to the bungalow. Now that all the parking space in the town was not swallowed up by holidaymakers she could have come to the shop in her car but she was in the habit of walking. The walking was good for her as she spent so many hours in the shop.

She didn't hurry home. What was there to hurry for? She had all the time in the world. She was cosy in her warm coat and walked around the shops first, some of which were

143

already decorated for Christmas. She would have to stay with her mother until after Christmas, it wouldn't be fair to leave them in the middle of the festive season. " I wonder what I'll be doing this time next year," she thought, as she was gathering ideas for decorating their shop.

She stopped to look at some of the paintings in the art shops. They had always fascinated her and since she had known Justin they fascinated her even more. She had always thought of artists being ' way out ' types but would never think so again. They were serious-minded people and the deeper they felt the more depth and character there was in their work. Perhaps if was those who were not good at art and would like to be who thought it would help if they dressed and behaved like most people's impression of the artists.

When she felt the pangs of hunger she realized that she had had nothing to eat all day in the shop because Justin hadn't been in to bring her anything. She had relied upon him lately to bring in food to keep them both going until they could have something substantial in the evening when their work was finished. She couldn't help thinking it was strange that Justin had stayed away from her so long for even the first day he had started work on his oil painting he had had to snatch a short time from it to come and see her in the evening. Perhaps he was producing a masterpiece which he couldn't possibly leave.

She arrived at the bungalow warm and rosy-cheeked and when she walked up the drive she stared, feeling unable to believe the evidence of her eyes. On the drive in front of the house stood a very familiar car. It was Mark's.

She told herself it couldn't possibly be, but who else did they know who was likely to own a luxury type car like that, the same colour as Mark's too. She had to stand for a moment to let her racing pulses settle down, and then, feeling she was almost composed, she went round the back and let herself in at the kitchen door.

144

Her mother was busy in the kitchen and when she saw Leonie her face lit up. " Oh, there you are, dear. You have a visitor."

" Mark," whispered Leonie. " What's he here for?"

" I don't know," said her mother. " You'd better go and find out, hadn't you? He's in the lounge. He hasn't long arrived and wanted to go down to the shop for you but I said you were due in any minute and he might miss you on the way. But you're later than I expected you to be."

" I've been walking round the town looking in shop windows," she said, talking to her mother to regain her self-control.

Mark couldn't have heard her come in. The television had been switched on for him to watch while he was waiting for Leonie so she slipped into her room to tidy herself before going in to see him.

She didn't change out of her slacks and jumper making it too obvious that she was doing herself up for him, but she brushed her hair, pushed it and coaxed it to look its best. She gave herself a spray of her most expensive perfume and for a long moment looked at herself in the mirror, giving long deep breaths to give herself control over her emotions.

" I'm stupid to get myself in this state," she thought. " He has probably had to call this way to see someone on business again and decided to call here before going back. She reminded herself that he had called her a two-timing cheat on the last occasion she had been with him in the lounge, and told herself she would not, under any circumstances allow herself to be carried away again. She wished she didn't have to keep seeing him. How could she get over him if she had to meet him again like this?

Her mother had seemed to have a secret little smile on her face as if she knew something. Could it be that Mark had been talking to her confidentially and her mother had told him how much her daughter had been grieving for him? Had he been desperate to see her again after their passionate kisses?

She turned from her mirror and left the room, walking to the lounge with a look, which she hoped, was calm, cool and collected.

TEN

Mark rose from the settee when she entered and she spoke in a voice with hardly a quiver in it. " Hello, Mark. Are you down here on business again so soon?"

" No," he said. " I came to see you."

" Oh?" she was surprised. " Why did you want to see me?"

" To talk to you."

She thought he looked a bit confused. Not at all sure of himself, which was unusual for Mark.

" Is there anything to say after what you said to me the last time you were here?" she asked.

He saw her cold, hard expression and turned away, going over to the window and looking out although it was dark and he wouldn't see a thing.

Without turning to look at her he said, " Do you remember what I said to you when you gave me back your engagement ring?"

" Yes," she said. " You told me I could have it back whenever I wanted it."

Why was he reminding her of that? She supposed he wanted to tell her it was no use asking for it now because he was going to marry someone else, but he needn't have come all this way to tell her that, surely. They both knew the wedding had been called off and he was free to marry anyone else when he chose to do so.

He turned to look at her now. " You never asked for it back again," he said.

She shrugged and said, " Did you expect me to humble

147

myself to you?"

He looked startled. "Humble yourself? Oh, Leonie, darling! Don't you know how I wanted you to ask me to return it?"

"But it's too late now."

"Is it? I could buy you a better one than this now," he said, bringing the ring from his pocket.

"Oh, no! I wouldn't want a better one. I loved that ring. I missed it so much. It was much more than you could afford at the time, but you insisted on buying it for me."

He took it from the little packet in which it was enclosed for she had the empty case herself, and he held it out to her. "Will you let me put it back where it belongs? Please?"

"You mean . . . Mark? . . ." she was afraid to believe he was asking her to become engaged to him again.

He held out his arms and with tears streaming down her face she went into them. "Oh, darling, am I dreaming?" she wept.

He held her so close she knew she wasn't dreaming, but he too, was too overcome for words. They clung to each other without kisses, and without words. It had been so long since they had become estranged, it was unbelievable joy to be together like this with no bitterness between them.

After a time he took her left hand and was fumbling to put the ring on her finger, through her own tears she could see that he was fumbling because his own eyes were full of tears too. But at last the ring was back on her finger, and he bent to press his lips against it. Then he kissed her. "Have you been as unhappy as I've been?" he asked.

"I've been unhappy, but you didn't seem to be," she said. "You were horrible when I came to the christening party."

"Well, I thought I was getting over you and suddenly you were there to remind me all over again."

"Mark," she said, between kisses, "why have we wasted the last two years?"

"Because we have been stupid idiots, especially me, I

148

suppose. When you gave me the ring back I didn't think you meant me to have it back permanently or I wouldn't have taken it back so easily. I would have begged you, pleaded with you to take it back. I knew you were in a temper and thought when you cooled down you would be glad to let me return it, and I didn't think anything when you said you could marry Eliot whenever you wanted. I thought that was just to make me change my mind. I was so sure that when you'd got over the disappointment of having to postpone the wedding you would realize that it was a marvellous opportunity for me, and one we couldn't afford not to take if we wanted a good future for ourselves, and our children. It was a great disappointment for me too you know, to have to put the wedding off. I was longing for us to be married as much as you were, but there was no time for anything. This opportunity had to be snatched or lost. When I came to your house the next evening and your mother said you were out with Eliot, it was as if you'd plunged a knife into my heart.

" I can't tell you how I felt when I left England. I was like someone bereaved. I wrote to you to tell you I had a dishy secretary to console me simply to let you know my address and in the hope that you'd reply and tell me you missed me, but you never wrote once."

" Your letter seemed to be telling me that you didn't care about losing me that's why I never wrote to you."

" I suppose it did. I wouldn't admit to you how hurt I was. After a time I concentrated on the work I'd been sent to do and all the time I hoped when I returned we might meet again and make it up if you weren't already married to Eliot, but when I returned they told me you'd sold your shop and gone to Cornwall. That seemed to me a deliberate decision to severe all connection with me. No one seemed to think it necessary to explain to me that you'd been compelled to sell your shop because the chemicals didn't suit your hands. It was only by chance that I discovered that, just before you were returning home from Paula's and it made me think.

149

Later, when we were looking at the photographs of you and the baby Paula asked me why we had broken our engagement and I told her what had happened and that you had told me you could marry Eliot any time you wanted, and the very next night after breaking off our engagement and returning the ring, you had gone out with Eliot, and she told me that you hadn't. You told her you didn't go out with him, you had just been trying to hurt me. So I decided to come and see you, making the excuse that I was bringing the snaps for you to see. I did have to see a man near Plymouth which was near enough for me to explain my being down your way. But when I saw you there was Justin."

"Oh, yes, Justin. But I don't love Justin."

"No, and he deserves your love more than I do. Do you know it was Justin who came to see me and told me you still loved me? He said you told him you couldn't ask for your ring back again."

"Justin! But how could he know how to get in touch with you?"

"He came round to see your mother while you were at the shop. She gave him the address of mum and dad, and they sent him to me."

"But she never told me," exclaimed Leonie.

"No. He asked her not to mention it in case nothing came of his visit. He said he loved you and wanted you himself but your happiness was more important than his own. If he had discovered that I wasn't interested in you any more he said he was going to make you love him. He'd never stop trying to win your love. But he had to know for sure, first, whether I loved you or not, because you were under the impression I was going to marry someone else. If that had been my intention you would never have known he'd been to see me."

"Dear Justin. I wondered where he'd got off to. I haven't seen him for several days."

"He was pleading your cause, darling. Do you want to

150

change your mind now you know what a splendid person he is?"

" I've always known what a splendid person he is. I probably would have married him eventually but he would have been second best for me and that wouldn't have been fair to him. Aren't you ashamed now, that you made fun of him?"

" I'm ashamed of so many things. I was horrible about Justin because I was filled with jealousy and upset because my journey to see you had ended in disappointment. And I'm ashamed about the way I handled that quarrel. I should have convinced you of my love and understood that you were only behaving unreasonably because you were as disappointed as I was that we couldn't get married as soon as we planned. If I hadn't been so stupid in accepting your ring back when we quarrelled we should have been spared so much unhappiness. I was too cock-sure of you, I never dreamt you might turn to someone else, and was confident you'd be asking for your ring back the next time we met. I was shattered when I went round for you and you'd gone out. I thought you couldn't do that to me if you loved me, knowing I had to go abroad, and to be with Eliot too. It hasn't been pride since I came home that's stopped me telling you I wanted you. I didn't think I had any chance."

" You must have thought I wasn't worth loving."

" I remembered how much we had meant to each other. I couldn't forget that. I shall always be indebted to Justin for bringing us together again. I doubt whether I could have been as big-hearted as he's been. And when he told me you couldn't ask me for your ring I felt such a lousy swine for not offering it to you and telling you how much I wanted you to have it. I'd been hanging on to it when all the time you couldn't bring yourself to tell me how much you wanted it back again. I failed you miserably, didn't I?"

" People would never believe that two grown-up people like us could be so daft, would they?" said Leonie. " You told me that house you'd had built was waiting for your wife

151

and that you hoped to get married soon."

He laughed. " I wasn't going to admit to you that I hadn't anyone interested enough in me to become my wife."

" I can't believe that," she said.

" I decided to have that house built and take out a mortgage because as a single man the taxation on my wages has been terrific, but with a mortgage I get income tax relief. I wanted a home of my own, though I hadn't decided on a wife. I didn't seem to take to anyone else."

" But what about Josy? Paula thought you'd either marry her or your secretary."

" Did she now?" he smirked. " Josy is the girl-friend of a young man we sent away to university and I've been taking her out, with his knowledge, because she was lonely without him. She had no family to turn to. My secretary, Jean, has often acted as hostess for me when I've been entertaining business people from abroad, but there's nothing more than friendship between us."

Mrs. Drew came to the door and without entering called, " Are you two coming for something to eat?"

" Yes," answered Leonie, and to Mark she said, " I was starving when I was on the way home, but you made me forget all about being hungry."

He held her close in his arms again and it was quite half an hour before they could come back to earth and think about anything so mundane as eating.

They couldn't keep her mother waiting any longer so she took his hand to draw him into the dining-room. Before they reached it he stopped her. " Will you come with me and see the house? If you like it we can move in as soon as you like."

" Without a marriage ceremony?" she asked, pretending to be shocked.

" Yes, if you want to," he said, smiling at her. " We can soon arrange for a wedding to take place."

Her mother and Aunt Louise were delighted to know that

Leonie and Mark were engaged again, the ring was sparkling on her finger. " You knew that Justin had gone to see Mark for me and never told me," accused Leonie.

" He asked us not to in case nothing came from it, though I had no doubt that you loved each other. I could tell when you were together last time and could have knocked your heads together when you parted again without making it up," said her mother. " That's why we started making plans right away for taking over your shop. We knew you would be selling it and we should miss it."

" And you were going round the world Justin told me," said Mark laughing, and holding her tightly round the waist. " He said he intended to go with you if you went."

" And now I won't be able to go," pouted Leonie, pretending she was disappointed.

" How awful it would have been if you'd gone," said Mark, seriously.

The next few weeks were like a wonderful dream for Leonie. She went back with Mark to see the house he had built and she loved it, though it definitely needed a woman's touch. It was obviously the home of a bachelor. Only half of it was furnished and that in a haphazard sort of way so Leonie had her work cut out to make the house into a beautiful home.

Mark allowed her to do just as she liked and was thrilled with the results. Paula was delighted to have her best friend back in the neighbourhood and Leonie was glad to discuss things with her and sought her advice on lots of things concerning the furnishing of the house.

Mark's parents were happy to know that Mark and Leonie were together again for they had been most upset for their son when they knew the engagement had been broken off. Although Leonie had loved Cornwall, and regretted that she was leaving her mother there, she felt more at home in the Midlands where she knew so many people, and felt she belonged here.

The wedding was planned to take place at Christmas and Leonie was rushed off her feet. She went back to Cornwall to collect her belongings and made final arrangements about the take-over of the shop. Mark told her to let her mother have it for much less than she had originally intended. " We don't need the money, love," he told her.

Now that she was back again with Mark she could hardly bear the short parting from him to return to Cornwall but he couldn't get any more time from work at that time. She loved him even more now than she'd done two years ago for he was even more loving towards her than he'd been then, treating her as someone very special. They had so very nearly lost each other so that now their love was even stronger than it had ever been.

Back in Cornwall she met Fran again and invited her and Angela to be her bridesmaids. Of course they were delighted though Leonie was not prepared to allow them to wear their own choice of dresses. She chose them herself, three-tiered pink floral dresses in very flimsy material which made them look so much more beautiful than the monstrosities they would have chosen themselves.

Of Justin, Leonie could learn nothing. No one knew where he was and she did so want to see him to thank him for all he'd done for her. It was most upsetting not to know where he was, even, and Fran looked pale and dejected, though she knew she had never stood a chance with him.

Leonie couldn't help having him on her mind, she so wanted him to be happy as she was. They received a wedding present from him that made her cry. He enclosed a letter to tell her he didn't know when the wedding would be but he knew it would be soon, and he sent her what he thought she might like to have. It was the oil painting of the fishermen done from those wonderful sketches he had shown her in the shop. She and Mark studied the painting and knew it was always be their greatest treasure. " It's beautiful," breathed Leonie, and there were tears pouring down her cheeks.

The picture took pride of place on the most prominent wall in their lounge which had been re-arranged to Leonie's liking. She had changed the curtains and most of the furniture, thankful that Mark liked the finished result saying he'd known there was something not quite right about the way it looked before.

Her mother and Aunt Louise, Fran and Angela came to the Midlands for the Christmas wedding which was a very smart affair and Leonie looked absolutely radiant. " You looked younger than you did the first day I met you," Mark told her, " and far more beautiful."

They had a short honeymoon in the south of France, spent a couple of nights in Paris and were then anxious to get back to the lovely home that was awaiting them.

" I wish you were coming to live in it for the first time as I am," she told Mark. " I'm so thrilled to be coming to my new home."

" It's never felt like a real home to me, Leonie, until now," he told her. " It was just a place where I lived. It gave me no great pleasure when I had no one to share it with. You have made it come alive for me, and I'm just as eager as you are to start really living in it."

In the spring she was delighted to have a letter from her mother to say that Justin had been to see her and wanted to know if he could work in her shop again as he'd done the previous summer. " Of course I was only too delighted to agree," wrote her mother, " and Fran is over the moon."

And then one evening Mark and Leonie had been sitting watching television when out of the blue came the announcement that there was to be an interview with Justin Lewis the famous artist who was at present living in Cornwall.

It seemed that Justin had been quite famous before he ever came to spend his days sketching in Leonie's shop but he had never told anyone. He had modestly claimed to have sold many of his paintings but had never mentioned the price he could demand for them and it seemed he was becoming even more famous.

He was seen sitting on the sea wall sketching early holiday-makers, and close to him Fran could be seen looking on. Leonie was so excited she could hardly contain herself.

" I shall begin to think you were in love with that fellow after all," smiled Mark, sitting there with his arm around her.

" Oh, I loved him," said Leonie, " but not in the way I love you. Without you my life isn't worth a thing."

He drew her close and she sat with her head against his shoulder as they watched the scene change and Justin was now working on a landscape scene with his easel up, and the camera moved in to show him putting in a touch here and there until the picture gradually came to life.

Justin in check shirt and jeans, his hair and his beard thick and dark as ever. He seemed calm and serene as he talked to the interviewer about his work and his successes. Leonie was so glad he loved his work so much and hoped it was some compensation for not winning her love.

Then the camera moved lovingly over some of Justin's most recent paintings, lingering on the beauty of each one, while the interviewer commented on the skill of the artist. He had been commissioned to do portraits for well-known people in Society and his pictures hung in several galleries. Justin had been very modest. Leonie had no idea he was so well known. Her gaze rose to the painting of the fishermen he had sent to them and she saw that Mark was looking at it too. They were proud to own a painting by Justin, given to them as a wedding present, and Leonie felt it was the finest one he had ever done.

She and Mark felt they had been married years when they went down to Cornwall in the summer. The two years they had been separated seemed to have faded into the past and it seemed they had never been parted.

They went to the gift shop where her mother and Aunt

Louise were still working. The shop was being run most efficiently, just as they had always run their homes. Justin was in his corner just as Leonie remembered him, and people were queueing to have their portrait done by him. He looked up from his sketching and saw them standing there and gave them a casual smile as he continued with what he was doing. Swiftly he finished the portrait which delighted the sitter, and then excusing himself for a moment he came to shake hands with Mark and give Leonie a kiss on her cheek. " You look blooming, Mrs. Trueman," he smiled.

" Thanks to you," she said.

He dismissed that as nothing and telling his waiting clients he would be engaged for a short time he invited Mark and Leonie to come outside and sit in the sun while they talked.

" We saw you on television," said Leonie. " We were very proud to think we knew you."

" I was very proud to be considered important enough to be invited to do that for the B.B.C.," he said. He looked at Leonie, keenly. " I can see that married life suits you fine," he said. " You've never looked so beautiful."

" I'm glad you came back to the shop," she said. " It was awful not knowing where you were. Do you see much of Fran."

He smiled, not sadly at all. " You'll be glad to know that Fran and I are going to be married," he said.

" Justin! I'm so glad," said Leonie.

" Yes, I'm taking her under my wing," he said. " She's a good writer you know, but it will take years before she ever makes any money at it. And Angela didn't get that novel accepted. At least no one's taken it yet, after all the work she did on it last year. I was so sorry for the girls. They were talking of going back to their parents and taking regular jobs. I knew that would have broken their hearts. I thought it such a shame they couldn't continue doing what they love doing so I asked Fran to marry me. As my wife she will be

157

able to devote all her time to writing if she wants to and she won't have to worry about making sufficient money to keep herself. Angela will live with us for the time being so that she can have a good chance to write without financial problems. They will either work it out of their systems or become successful one day," he said.

"And they won't have to work at all? Mother will miss them I daresay."

"They've agreed to help your mother and your aunt in the shop, Leonie, during the busy periods, but those two women seem to be able to cope extremely well. You'd think they'd been in business all their lives."

Just then Fran came along and her eyes sparkled as she looked at Justin with such love in her eyes. She clearly idolized him and he seemed to find her adoration somewhat amusing. "I'll leave you to talk to Fran now," he said, rising from the sea wall so that she could take his place. "I must get back to my clients, I shall need all the money I can get when I'm married," he grinned.

Fran gave Leonie a big hug. "I'm so happy," she said, "Justin's absolutely marvellous to me."

"I hope you'll be as happy as Mark and I are," said Leonie.

Later Mark and Leonie strolled along the cliff tops overlooking the sea which was so calm and beautiful, sparkling in the sunshine. They watched the surf-riders, the sunbathers and the swimmers. The seagulls were screeching overhead.

"I'm so glad for Justin and Fran," said Leonie. "Justin will be happy with her, don't you think so?"

"I sincerely hope so, darling," said Mark, "though I'm sure he'll always feel he's missed out in not having you. It makes me feel very grateful that you wanted me when you could have had a fine man like Justin."

He pulled her into his arms to kiss her and she seemed to be at one with the blue skies, the shimmering ocean, and the crying seagulls. Completely in harmony with nature and everything else because she was with the one she loved. Without Mark she was only half alive, that she knew from experience, she needed him to make life perfect. And by the look in his eyes as they met hers she knew the same went for him too, he needed her to make his life perfect.

As they strolled on hand in hand looking out across the beautiful bay she sent up a silent prayer of thanksgiving for all her happiness and she added another little prayer for Justin and Fran, hoping that Justin would be happy with Fran, for he would always have a special place in Leonie's heart.

" You look very solemn," said Mark, smiling down at her.

" I'm overwhelmed with happiness," she said, and found his hand gripping hers more firmly.

" I know that feeling," he murmured, and there was no mistaking the love in his eyes as they met hers.